The
PUPPETEER'S
APPRENTICE

The

PUPPETEER'S
APPRENTICE

D. Anne Love

Margaret K. McElderry Books
NEW YORK • LONDON • TORONTO • SYDNEY • SINGAPORE

For Emma

MARGARET K. MCELDERRY BOOKS
An imprint of Simon & Schuster Children's Publishing Division
1230 Avenue of the Americas
New York, New York 10020
Copyright © 2003 by D. Anne Love
Book design by Russell Gordon
The text of this book is set in Tiepolo.
Printed in the United States of America
2 4 6 8 10 9 7 5 3 1
Library of Congress Cataloging-in-Publication Data
Love, D. Anne
The puppeteer's apprentice / D. Anne Love.
p. cm.
Includes bibliographical references.
Summary: A medieval orphan girl called Mouse gains the courage she
needs to follow her dreams of becoming a puppeteer's apprentice.
ISBN 0-689-84424-7
[1. Puppets—Fiction. 2. Orphans—Fiction. 3. Middle Ages—Fiction.
4. England—Fiction.] I. Title.
PZ7.L9549 Pu 2003
[Fic]—dc21   2001044868

FIRST
EDITION

Contents

→ CHAPTER ONE ←

An Ending

Long ago and far away, on a morning that was not quite winter and not quite spring, Lord and Lady Dunston bade all who lived at the manor to a gathering in the great hall. The farriers and stableboys, the dairymaids with their pails, the weavers and spinners and serving girls set aside their work and hurried along the stone corridors, gossiping all the way. Mayhap Lord Dunston was off to war again, they whispered. Mayhap his lady soon would bring forth a new child.

When the summons reached the kitchen, Cook dropped his spoons and mopped his shiny red face. "Make haste, Fenn," he said to the terret-faced baker, who was at that moment taking a loaf of bread from the fire. "We must not keep them waiting."

The scullery maid, a skinny, sad-eyed girl in a dirt-brown tunic, gazed longingly at the golden loaf, her belly tight with hunger. But the bread was not meant for the likes of her. She ignored her rumbling stomach and hurriedly tossed the turnips she'd just peeled into the black kettle bubbling in the hearth. In all her years at Dunston Manor, she had caught only fleeting glimpses of the lord and his lady. Her days were spent peeling onions, washing pots, and carrying Fenn's pastries from hearth to table. At night she slept on the stone floor among the fleas and vermin, surrounded by the odd bits of beauty she had collected in her short and somber life—a scrap of purple ribbon rescued from a branch in the orchard, a blue glass bead found on the path to the privy, a sliver of polished metal that gave back her reflection, large dark eyes in a thin and determined face.

Sometimes, when Cook was too busy to notice her absence, she stole away to her hiding place near the solar. There, with her ear pressed firmly to the damp wall, she listened to snippets of conversations of the serving girls and chambermaids, to the tales of passing visitors, or to the solemn voice of some visiting priest reading from a holy book—wishing she could read such comforting stories for herself, wishing she had someone with whom she could share her secrets, wishing *she* might travel to faraway places. But she was not thinking such thoughts today.

Today, something important was astir, and she longed to be a part of it.

"Not you, Mouse!" Cook cried when he saw the expectant look on her face. "Stay here and tend this pot. And clear those turnip peels off the floor. If Lord Dunston's news has aught to do with you, you will know it soon enough."

Taking up his flesh hook, he poked the slab of venison simmering in its soup of leeks and cabbage. "See this meat does not burn, else there will be the devil to pay."

"Drat!" the girl muttered. "Why must I be left behind to sweep and stir?"

"What?" Cook growled, mopping his face again.

"I merely said, 'Yes, sir.'"

Satisfied, Cook nodded, hung his apron on its peg beside the door, then set off toward the great hall, Fenn trotting like an obedient puppy at his heels.

Mouse intended to obey Cook, but the air of mysterious excitement permeating the very walls of the manor house, and her own considerable curiosity, soon overcame her better judgment. She gave the pot another stir, tossed more wood onto the fire, then scurried up the dark stone steps just in time to see Cook's ample rump, and Fenn's skinny one, disappearing down the corridor. Following at a safe distance, she hurried along the hallway, past the weaving room, then up more stairs, till she came to the tall doors guarding the great hall. There, she pressed herself into a dark corner.

Above the iron bolt, where the wooden door had split, was a crack just wide enough for Mouse to see everyone who had assembled behind long wooden tables where the morning meal had recently concluded. Mouse spied Cook and Fenn and the rosy-cheeked chambermaids, all whispering together. Lady Dunston's attendants stood by her side, resplendent in their embroidered gowns and headpieces. Lady Dunston herself wore a gown of blue velvet and a gold circlet on her head.

Lord Dunston tapped his silver-headed cane upon the floor, and the room went still.

"Lady Dunston and I are happy to announce the betrothal of our daughter, Penelope, to Sir Geoffrey of Fairfax," he said. Everyone applauded. From her hiding place in the shadows, Mouse clapped too.

"Where is Penelope?" one of the ladies asked. "Bring her here so that we may give her our good wishes."

"She is so overcome with joy, she has taken to her bed," Lord Dunston replied. "But a day of rest will put her to rights."

"Taken to her bed, is she?" murmured one of the serving girls to her companion. Mouse pressed closer to listen.

"She is overcome, but not with joy, I trow," the other replied. "Wrinkled as a prune, that Geoffrey is. Hair like a haystack. And none too bright, either, from the looks of him."

"But he owns half the land twixt here and the sea, or so they say," returned the first. "And Penelope is getting on in years herself. Twenty-three last summer, if I remember rightly. Lord Dunston is wise to arrange such a match before she is too old to be a wife to anyone."

Lord Dunston tapped his cane again. "The wedding will commence in a fortnight," he said. "You must begin preparations at once. Lady Dunston and I wish it to be the finest celebration in the realm."

A wedding! Such a celebration meant musicians with flutes and lyres and tambourines, or so Fenn said. Jesters there would be, and dancing and merriment and a feast fit for the king himself. Mayhap the lord and his lady would invite even Mouse, the lowest of the low. She would wear her purple ribbon and a flower in her hair. She must learn to curtsy, she thought, and to speak a proper greeting. A delicious shiver traveled down her spine.

Inside the great hall another round of cheering and applause erupted as the lord and his lady bowed their heads and took their leave by the doors at the far end of the hall. Then the door next to Mouse's hiding place opened, and everyone spilled out, laughing and chattering all at once. Mouse crouched in the shadows and waited for them to pass. She dared not show herself and risk Cook's vile temper. More than once he had cursed her, or cuffed her cheeks till her ears rang, for even the smallest of mistakes. If she dropped a bowl upon the floor or forgot to add salt to the bread, he called her an addlebrained clod, a muddleheaded lout, or worse. It was best to wait till the room was empty, then return to the kitchen through the far doors, well ahead of Cook and Fenn.

At last the hall was deserted. Mouse hastened inside, pulling the heavy door closed behind her.

If only she had kept to her plan, everything that happened later would not have happened at all. But as soon as she entered the hall, her gaze was fastened to the gleaming tapestries on the walls and she could not move. Colorful birds, angels, and flowers, scenes of knights on horseback and ladies in gardens seemed to spring to life before her eyes. She could almost hear the ladies talking quietly as they bent low over their needlework awaiting the knights' return. She could just imagine the stories the men would tell, stories of adventure and noble deeds performed in the service of the king.

Then on the long tables, amid empty goblets and a forest of candlesticks dripping wax, Mouse saw the remains of the morning meal. Here was a half-eaten meat pie and a bit of peacock, shiny with raisin sauce; there a morsel of fine white bread sticky with honey. Mouse's stomach rumbled, for her breakfast had been nothing more than a crust of stale bread and a bowl of cold cabbage, slick with grease. Almost before she knew it, she gobbled the last of the meat pie and a handful of figs and tucked another pie inside her tunic. On her way to the doors leading to the courtyard, she spied an apple tart and ate that, too, in three quick bites. She licked her fingers clean, then pushed open the doors and went out.

"You there! Stop!" A man carrying a bucket and a sack grabbed her arm and twisted so hard, Mouse yelped. The meat pie she had hidden in her tunic landed with a *plop* on the cobblestones. "Aha! Just as I suspected! Stealing from the poor."

It was the almoner, whose job it was to collect table scraps for the needy. Cook said such charity was one way the lord and his lady kept themselves in the good graces of the villagers.

"Leave me be!" Mouse yelled, struggling with all her might to break free. "I am no thief, but Cook's own helper."

Just then Cook appeared, brandishing his flesh hook. "So there you are, you miserable wretch! Did I not tell you to tend the meat? Now it is burned black as tar, and I will get the blame!"

The almoner tightened his grip on Mouse's arm. "She has stolen food, too. Right off the lord's own table.

Caught her, I did, stuffing herself like a Christmas goose, while the poor in the village have neither bread nor ale to stop their hunger." He glared at Mouse. "Mayhap I should take her to Lord Dunston. He will know how to deal with the likes of her."

"Lord Dunston has more important things on his mind," Cook said. "Leave her to me."

The almoner flung Mouse onto the hard cobblestones. "Next time I will flog you myself! Thief!"

He stomped into the great hall, his boots ringing on the stone steps.

"Well?" Cook loomed over the cowering Mouse.

"I am sorry." Mouse's voice trembled. Her stomach squeezed with fright. "I was hungry."

Behind her the kitchen door creaked open, and Fenn dumped the ruined venison into a slop pail, where it floated, black and crusty, among rotting turnips, browning apples, and gray meat full of squirming maggots.

"Hungry, are you?" Cook mocked. "And my bread and cabbage are not good enough, I suppose. You may be a mouse, but you have the manners of a pig!"

Before she could reply, he twisted her ear, jerked her to her feet, and propelled her toward the stinking slop pail. "Eat, pig!" he commanded, pushing her face into the pail.

"I will not!" Mouse pulled and squirmed, but try as she might, she could not free herself from Cook's viselike grasp.

"Oh, yes, you will." With his meat hook, he speared a slab of maggoty pork and pushed it into her face. "Eat, if you are so hungry. Eat every bite!"

Mouse's stomach pitched and roiled. Feeling hot and cold all at once, she twisted her head away, but not before spewing vomit over Cook's white apron and the tops of his shoes. Bits of meat pie clung to his hair, his eyelashes, his wiry black beard.

Bellowing with rage, he raised his meat hook and raked it savagely across Mouse's cheek. The spoiled meat fell to the ground.

At first she stood there, stunned, while a warm, sticky trickle of blood ran down her face. She wiped her cheek and stared at her bloody hand, too full of shock and fear to feel pain. Cook raised the meat hook again. But before he could land another blow, the wall of fear and loneliness that had been building inside Mouse all her life suddenly broke. And she ran. Across the rain-slick courtyard, then out through the great stone arch and over the newly plowed fields to the road.

"Stop her!" Cook yelled, but the planters did not hear and went on with their sowing and raking.

Mouse ran until the house disappeared from view. Then the pain began, so hot and fierce, it nearly stole her breath. But she went on until at last her legs buckled, and she stopped beside an icy stream. With the dampened hem of her tunic, she bathed her wound. As the cold water numbed her pain and her breathing slowed, the full weight of her plight filled her mind.

"Saints in heaven! What have I done now?" she said aloud.

Many times, after one of Cook's thrashings, she had thought of running away. Once she had actually tried it, but she'd soon been returned to the scullery. And mayhap it was just as well, for where could she go, a girl with nothing? No family. Not even a proper name.

Abandoned as a babe on the steps of Dunston Manor, she had been called Mouse all her life. She could not say how many twelvemonths had passed since her birth. Once, when she had begged Cook to tell her when and why she had come to Dunston Manor, he had said, in his exasperated way, that mayhap she was eleven. Or twelve. As to the reason she had been left to the mercy of strangers, Cook said it was obvious, was it not? She was not wanted. And no wonder. She was scrawny and ugly and clumsy as a cow. Not the kind of girl anyone was wont to keep. It was only at Lady Dunston's insistence that she had been taken into the scullery in exchange for her unceasing labor.

At first Mouse had refused to believe him. She imagined she was lost or had been left at Dunston by some horrid mistake that soon would be righted. At night, listening to the scrabbling of the rats in the kitchen, she pictured a beautiful princess with golden hair searching the realm for her lost daughter. But as time passed, each season sliding into the next, she realized such thoughts were useless and accepted her lot. At least she had a roof over her head and a scrap of food each day.

Now she was alone, without any prospects in the world, without a single coin in her pocket, nor anyone to help her. Lying on the ground while the cold wind tore at her thin tunic, Mouse felt exactly like her namesake, small and despised and unimportant. Another girl might have wept at the hopelessness of it, but Mouse had learned tears would not change anything.

"I will not cry," she said aloud to the shivering trees. With one hand pressed to her wounded cheek, she looked around for shelter from the cold rain that had begun to fall and at last burrowed into a pile of rotting leaves beside the road, where she passed a long, sleepless night.

The next morning the weather was still cold and damp, and Mouse was still hurt and alone. Her cheek throbbed. Her stomach felt as if it had stuck to her backbone, but there was nothing at all to eat. She broke the thin film of ice that had formed on the stream and filled her groaning belly. Then, because she had nothing to do and nowhere to go, she scurried back to her bed of leaves and lay there trying to decide what to do.

Presently an oxcart brimming with straw and cabbages trundled down the road. Mouse watched as the driver halted the cart and led the ox to drink, poking the ice with his staff till it broke with a faint tinkling sound. While he was busy, she stole into the cart and hid beneath the mound of dry straw. Still she had no plan for her future; she knew only that she could not go back to Dunston Manor.

The cart squeaked and shifted beneath the driver's weight. The ox snorted as the cart lurched along the road. Mouse poked a hole through the straw and breathed in the cold morning air. Beneath her fingers her wounded cheek oozed and burned fiercely, as if she had strayed too close to Cook's hearth.

She peered out across a field of brown stubble. Beneath a stand of rain-washed trees, two farmers were mending a stone fence. The cart rolled on, past a woman tending her geese, past a goat boy with his herd, past a man on a prancing horse.

Late in the morning Mouse spied in the distance a scattering of thatched roofs and a few stone buildings of a village. Her old life was at an end. A new one was beginning, though she could not yet imagine it.

→ CHAPTER TWO ←

The Travelers

Mouse clutched the sides of the cart as it climbed toward the village, the wheels creaking and groaning behind the plodding ox. Suddenly hoofbeats drummed on the road, then Mouse heard the startled whinny of a horse. A man shouted a curse.

The cart lurched, then pitched end over end into a deep ravine beside the road. Mouse felt herself flying through the air amid tumbling cabbages, heard the straw rustle beneath her weight as she hit the ground. Then the world went black.

When she revived, the cart and driver were gone, but she was not alone. Voices came to her as she lay in the ravine, eyes closed, her head throbbing.

"She is not dead!" a woman said. "God be praised."

"Poor thing," said another woman with a softer voice. "An orphan, I would reckon by the looks of her.

Why, she is thin as a rake. And that tunic! I have seen beggars in finer clothes than that."

"Stand back, ladies!" This voice belonged to a man. Slowly, Mouse opened her eyes. He was tall and reed-like, with moss-green eyes and a mouth that looked as if it had smiled forever.

"Well, now," he said to Mouse. "You are alive at that! Can you sit up?"

"I think so." Mouse struggled to right herself, but everything turned upside down in a hot, black swirl, and she lay back on the straw.

"Quickly!" the woman with the louder voice said. "Help her."

The man lifted Mouse from the ravine and laid her gently beside the road. "Sweet Satan! What happened?" he asked, taking in her matted hair, bloodstained tunic, and dirty feet.

Mouse shook her head, afraid to trust him despite his kindly eyes.

"No matter. Whatever their cause, your wounds must be tended." He opened a leather pouch, took out a jar, and smoothed something cool and greasy onto her cheek. It smelled worse than the piggery at Dunston Manor, but soon it took the pain away. Mouse sat up, watching as the man stirred some dried leaves into a flask of water.

"Drink this," he said.

She sniffed it cautiously.

"It will not hurt you. 'Tis only a bit of blessed thistle, the best cure in the world for all our earthly ailments. Drink it, then you shall have something to eat."

The promise of food was all the encouragement Mouse needed. She drank the bitter concoction, then eyed the bread and apples the man had taken from his pouch.

"Sit here, child." The loud-voiced woman was nearly as tall as the man, with a sweep of black hair and bare feet coated with tar. She gave Mouse a fat apple and drew her close.

Mouse munched her apple and studied the other woman. Her eyes were a deep clear blue, the color Mouse imagined the sea might be. Her hair was the color of fresh butter, and her hands were dainty and milk-white, like those of the ladies in the cloth pictures at Dunston Manor. Though she smiled, she wore sorrow like a cloak, as if something deep and sad had settled inside her. Just as Mouse was wondering what had happened to trouble her so, the woman spoke.

"Where are you going, child?" she asked in a voice as lovely as her face.

"I cannot say." Mouse broke off a bit of bread and chewed it slowly.

"You are wise to be wary of strangers on the road,"

said the tar-footed woman. "But we mean you no harm. Otherwise, we would not have rescued you."

"Tell us your story," the man urged. "It will be a hot day in January before you find more sympathetic ears."

And then, because she was hurt and alone in the world, Mouse told the three travelers everything. How she had been left as a helpless babe on the steps of the manor house, and how Cook had named her Mouse and taught her to fetch and carry, stir and knead, sweep and peel. How she had stolen into the great hall—was it only yestermorn?—and eaten the forbidden food. "So you see," she finished, "I know not where to go, nor what will become of me."

"Dear me," the man mused. "Yours is indeed a sad tale and your problem much too big for solving in a single afternoon. Here is what I propose: We three are on our way to York, which is some days' walk from these parts. Come with us, and by journey's end mayhap we will have hit upon some plan."

"Do come," the two women chorused.

"We dare not leave you on this road alone," said the one with tarred feet. "Not with robbers about."

"They would get naught from me," Mouse declared. "For I have nothing but this tattered tunic and an aching head."

"All the more reason to join our company," the man said cheerfully. "Permit me to make the introductions. This," he said, indicating the dark-haired woman, "is Alice. From Depford. A goose woman by trade, as you can plainly tell from the tar upon her feet. The other is Claire, most recently from Trumpington, but who has decided to seek her fortune in York. And I am Simon Swann. Music maker, juggler, and minstrel. As you wish."

The two women clapped as Simon swept into a low bow. Then he took out his lute. "I shall make a soothing song whilst you eat," he said, "and we shall speak no more of your sad plight, for an unquiet meal makes for ill digestion."

Alice draped a blanket about Mouse's shoulders. Claire brought water from the stream. Then the travelers encircled Mouse. Claire and Simon sang while Mouse ate her fill.

When Mouse had eaten all the bread and nibbled the apple right down to the core, Simon stood. "The day grows short, and we must be away," he said. "Come along, Mouse. You seem a well-spoken child, but I do not care one farthing for your name. Mayhap on this journey we shall choose a new one for you."

They gathered their bundles and set off down the road. Winter's bitterness was waning; the sun warmed the air, and a gentle breeze settled softly on Mouse's face. Here and there, fuzzy green buds sprouted on the trees and a few violets poked their heads above the brown grasses. With her stomach full and the three travelers for company, Mouse began to feel better.

"This day reminds me of an old Maysong," Simon said. He strummed his lute and sang.

"When first the leaves are green upon the trees,
And bees in the newborn blossoms buzz,
When the sun shines bright and sweet birdsong fills the
*   wood,*
Then does my heart sing for joy."

When he finished, everyone clapped, Mouse loudest of all.

"That was lovely, Simon," Claire said. "Never have I heard a sweeter tune or a more agreeable voice."

"My thanks, fair lady. Now it is your turn."

Claire's laughter was a clear, sweet sound, like chimes. "Oh ho! You know not what you ask, Simon. Pigs in the sty sing more sweetly than I."

"You are too modest," Simon said. "But all right. Mayhap Alice will favor us with some tune."

"My song would frighten every creature in the

wood," Alice said. "But I will make you a riddle to speed the day along."

"A riddle!" Simon exclaimed. "Are you listening, Mouse?"

Still astonished at how quickly her fortune had turned, Mouse could only nod.

"All right," Alice began. "Here it is. What is the bravest thing in all the world?"

"A knight," Claire said promptly.

"No!" Alice said, laughing. "Your turn, Mouse."

"A lion?" Mouse guessed, remembering Fenn's stories of the fierce beasts that could swallow a man's head in a single bite.

"A good try, but no," Alice said. "Simon? What say you?"

"Bravest thing in all the world." He scratched his head. "The husband of a shrewish wife, no doubt."

"Wrong!" Alice whooped. "The answer is: a miller's shirt. For every day it grasps a thief by the throat."

Her companions howled gleefully, but Mouse frowned with puzzlement. Simon explained. "Everyone in the village must bring his grain to the miller for grinding. Since he is the only one who can do the job, he is free to cheat everyone, and usually does. He is the most unpopular man in the village, and the richest one as well."

On they walked for some distance before Simon said,

"Claire? Since you will not sing for us, tell us another riddle."

"I know no riddles," Claire said dolefully.

"What? No riddles? No songs? What manner of woman are you?"

"Leave her be," Alice said.

But Simon persisted. "It is a long way to York. Tell us anything Claire, a story or a poem. Anything at all to speed this tedious journey."

"A poem, then," Claire said, sighing. "A very old one I learned when I was no older than you, Mouse.

*"Upon the dawn-lit plain, knights and chargers are
    arrayed
Their shields and swords gleaming.
The trumpet sounds.
The battle begins, the vassals go down together.
Maces, helmets, lancers, and chargers scattered
Upon the ground.
While in the castle a maiden waits,
A prayer upon her lips."*

Alice dabbed at her eyes. "A goodly poem, but too sad."

"Yes," Claire said. "It always makes me weep."

Eager to dispel the gloom that had settled over them,

Mouse said to Simon, "If you please, sing another song."

"Indeed," Alice agreed. "Something to lift our spirits, Simon, if it be not too much trouble."

"Later," Simon said. "For now it is Mouse's turn to entertain us with some tale."

"Until yestermorn I had seen naught save the fields and forests of Dunston," Mouse said. "I have no tales to tell."

"Pish and tosh! If you will think but a moment, I am certain some amusing story will come to mind."

Mouse chewed her lip and thought. At last she said, "Once I stole a horse, though that was not my intent."

"You? A thief?" Claire said. "I do not believe it."

"Do tell!" Alice urged.

"Yes," Simon agreed, "for I would learn how one steals a horse without intending to."

"It was near Midsummer's Eve," Mouse said, "when a coach bearing Lady Dunston's cousins turned up the drive and Cook set me to peeling onions for soup."

"An odious task," Alice said.

"Not to me," Mouse said. "I had not eaten since early morning, and the onions seemed sweeter than cake. Before I knew it, I had eaten a whole bowl of them. Cook caught me just as I was swallowing the last bite."

"Dear me," Simon said.

"He beat me with his fist and said he would tell Lady Dunston of my thievery as soon as supper was finished. I was afraid, and as soon as his back was turned, I ran."

"Yes, yes, but what of the horse?" Simon said. "I am nearly faint with curiosity."

"When I reached the courtyard, I saw the peddler's horse standing near the gate. He had a fat pack on his back. I was still hungry, so I climbed onto the stirrup to see if there was food I could take for my journey. Before I could open the pack, the horse bolted. I could not catch the reins, so I held on to his mane."

"You might have been killed!" Claire said.

"I was afraid," Mouse admitted. "He ran and ran and jumped the fence down by the privy. We went tearing through the wood, with me clinging like a burr to his side, one leg in the stirrup and the other sticking up like a flagpole."

The three travelers laughed. Mouse grinned. At the time she had been terrified, but now, with her new friends as an audience, the whole thing seemed more like an adventure than an ordeal.

"Go on," Simon said when he had recovered his breath.

"I looked back, and the peddler was running after me, yelling, 'Stop, thief!' But I could not stop. The horse jumped a stream, and I fell off. He kept going."

"Were you hurt?" Alice asked, wiping her eyes.

"Only some bruises and a lump on my head. I was too afraid to go back to Dunston. I hid in the wood, but before I could think of what to do, Fenn found me and took me back. Cook was so busy, he forgot to tell Lady Dunston about the onions and he never knew I had run away."

"You went back to that evil man," Claire said.

"I had nowhere else to go," Mouse said simply.

"But now you are off on a grand adventure!" Simon said. "And I shall sing us another song. A happy song is just what we need. Too much sadness will surely congeal our blood."

And so the first day passed.

When darkness fell, they slept in a hamlet close by the road in a tanner's stall. The air was thick and stale, and the hides covering them were stiff with hair and dried blood, but Mouse slept soundly.

Shortly before sunrise Simon woke them, and they stole onto the road again, not stopping till the sun had climbed above the trees and the village lay far behind. Then he opened his pack and took out bread, honey, and a slab of fresh roasted pork.

"Where did you get all this, pray tell?" Alice asked.

"Here and there," he replied with a wave of his hand.

Mouse did not care where Simon had gotten the food, for she was hungry, right down to the ends of her toes.

"I would have given the shopkeeper a goodly price, had the lazy lout once bestirred himself," Simon declared. "As it was, I left a poem in payment."

"A poem instead of a coin?" Alice scoffed.

"A man's soul must be fed as well as his belly," Simon said. "My poem will do him more good than another tankard of ale." He tore off a hunk of bread, dipped it into the honey, and handed it to Mouse. "How is your wound and your sore head, little Mouse?"

"Better." Eagerly, Mouse bit into the bread.

"And how is your sore heart today, sweet Claire?"

"I know not what you mean," Claire said.

"Oh, you take my meaning well enough," Simon said. "Pretending otherwise will not ease your sorrow."

Tears sprang to Claire's eyes. She stood up and ran down the road.

"Now see what you have done," Alice said angrily. She tossed her bread onto the blanket and ran after Claire.

"What makes Claire so sad?" Mouse asked. She finished her own bread and eyed the piece Alice had left behind.

"It is quite a complicated tale," Simon began. "Not more than a fortnight ago I arrived in Trumpington to sing for the folks thereabouts. They were tired of winter and ready for a diversion, and there I was with my lute and some new songs and a riddle or two. At Lord Boswick's house I met Claire, who was serving as companion to his daughter, Eleanor."

Mouse nodded. Lord Dunston's daughter, Penelope, had a companion too, an old woman with a face like a rotten apple and a disposition to match. Not one bit like Claire.

Simon went on. "As it happened, I arrived upon the very day Lord Boswick announced Eleanor's betrothal to Rupert Howard." He paused in his tale to lick away the honey that dribbled down his fingers. "Rupert is one slimy fellow, Mouse, for he had long ago professed his love for Claire. She thought they would marry as soon as his fortune was settled, but alas! His father died and left the house, all the land and the sheep, everything, to Rupert's younger brother. Unheard of!"

Mouse broke off a bit of Alice's bread, too small a piece to notice. She dipped it into the honey. "Then what happened?"

"An honorable man would have found a way to keep his promise, especially to a girl as lovely as Claire. But not Rupert. Without his inheritance, the only thing standing between him and utter ruin was Eleanor's considerable dowry, so he proposed marriage right away. But the joke will be on him soon enough, for a man who marries for wealth is sure to sell his happiness in the bargain."

"Poor Claire," Mouse said.

"Indeed." Simon looked thoughtful. "It is a bitter thing to look into happiness through another's eyes. It would have been quite impossible for Claire to go on living under the same roof with the one who had stolen all her dreams. So, when I was ready to take my leave, she asked if she might travel along in any direction I happened to fancy, and here we are."

Mouse pulled off another hunk of Alice's bread. "What will she do when we get to York?"

"I cannot say. I promised only to see her safely there. Then I must be away to London to sing at the fair."

"Fenn says London is the finest place in all the world. Mayhap I will go with you."

Simon laughed. "If you were a boy, you would make a goodly companion, for already you have grown on me like an old tune. But the life of a minstrel is no life at all for a maid like you."

Mouse dared not argue, but she determined to change Simon's mind. The sheer, wild freedom of the open road was everything. She liked seeing new places, sleeping in a different town each night. She liked telling stories and singing songs. Mayhap in London she would find a way to make a life of her own in the world.

She pictured the look on Cook's face when he entered the scullery to find she had not come back. She imagined him getting further and further behind in his work because she was not there to help him. She imagined potatoes and turnips and onions piling up to the ceiling, and dirt lying ankle-deep on the stone floor because she was not there to sweep. It gave her pleasure to think of it.

Alice and Claire returned. Simon handed Claire a piece of bread, dripping with honey. "Forgive me, dear Claire. I hereby vow to hold my tongue for the rest of this journey, else you may cut it out of my head and roast it for your supper."

Claire smiled, a bit sadly, Mouse thought. "I would not exact so dear a price. You may keep your tongue, Simon."

"My bread!" Alice exclaimed. "I left it right here, and now it is gone."

"Oh!" Mouse gasped at the mound of crumbs littering the blanket, all that remained of Alice's bread. She had not forgotten what had happened the last time she dared to eat her fill. But Alice merely laughed. "It seems a little mouse has stolen a meal. But no matter. I like meat as well as bread."

She dipped a piece of pork in the honey and popped it into her mouth. Then she licked her lips and said to Mouse, "So. You come from Dunston. I imagine all is astir there, now that Penelope is finally to wed."

Mouse was astonished. "How did you know?"

Simon said, "Alice knows everyone and everything that happens hereabouts. Truly, she is a walking history book, or else the most accomplished gossip in all of northern England. Whichever is the truth, if you want to know anything at all, Mouse, you have only to ask Alice."

"I cannot help it," Alice said, swirling another bit of meat into the honey. "Once I hear something, it sticks inside my head like glue, whether I want it to or not."

Simon wiped his hands and put away his pouch. Alice hastily chewed the last of her pork. Soon the travelers were on their way again.

When they stopped in midafternoon to drink from a rushing stream, Claire suddenly said, "Turn your back, Simon. I wish to have a bath."

"In that water? You will turn to a block of ice."

"I am accustomed to it, and besides, it does not feel so cold once you are in it." She smiled at Mouse. "Forgive me, little one, but you could do with a bath as well."

"And so could I," Alice decided. "Come along, Mouse. It will not be so bad. The sun will keep us warm."

"You have taken leave of your senses," Simon said calmly. "But all right. If you wish to waste time, who am I to complain? Mayhap I will go in search of our supper."

Before Mouse could say a word, Alice and Claire disappeared behind a bush, shed their clothes, then plunged, whooping, into the stream. They bobbed side by side, with only their heads and pale shoulders showing above the water.

"Come on in, Mouse!" Claire called. "And bring your tunic. It could do with a washing as well."

Mouse dipped one foot into the icy water. The cold made her toes tingle.

Alice laughed. "It is best to jump in all at once."

But Mouse, who had never before gone swimming, cautiously waded in till the water covered her knees. Her teeth chattered. Suddenly something closed around her ankle. She fell backward into the water and came up shivering and sputtering.

Claire bobbed up beside her, grinning. "Forgive me, Mouse, but you must admit this is much better, is it not?"

And it was true that Mouse soon forgot the cold. What a strange and wondrous feeling it was, drifting on the water like a feather, lazy as a cloud in a bright blue sky. Alice splashed and swam in the shallows. Claire floated, eyes closed against the sun, her hair spread out like a yellow lily pad, her knees sticking up like two small white islands in the green water. The two women seemed to have forgotten all their cares, but Mouse was full of more questions than ever.

"Is it true?" she asked Alice. "Are you a walking history book?"

The goose woman wiped water from her eyes. "I hear stories when I am on the road or in the markets with my geese. And I have a good memory, true enough."

"I am wondering," Mouse said, "how I came to live at Dunston Manor. I want to know how old I am. Do you know about my mother?"

"Ah, child. I wish it were so, but yours is a story I have not heard. You must not dwell on it. The future is more important than the past. Now, give me your tunic."

Mouse lifted her arms, and Alice helped her out of the tunic. From a small pouch around her neck, Alice took a sliver of hard, black soap and gave Mouse's tunic a thorough scrubbing. Claire soaped her own hair, then Mouse's, and when they were clean, they climbed out of the water. Alice spread Mouse's tunic on a bush to dry. Claire tossed Mouse her white linen undergarment. "Wear my chemise till your tunic is dry."

They dressed and sat on the riverbank, drying their hair in the sun. Mouse leaned against Claire's shoulder, listening to the two women's quiet talk. If only this golden afternoon could go on forever, with the three of them at the center of it.

Soon Simon returned, bearing two fat hares for their supper. While Claire and Alice kindled a fire, he skinned the game and set it to roasting on the spit. When they were seated around the fire, he nodded approvingly. "That bath was worth our time after all, for our little Mouse has turned into a queen."

Mouse blushed. "I am naught but a skinny maid with a wounded face."

"Your wound will heal," he said kindly. "In time you will take no more heed of it than your own breath."

With that, he unlaced his boot, took off his stocking, and wiggled his toes in the air.

"Simon!" Alice cried. "Whatever are you doing?"

He ignored her. "Look closely, Mouse. Does the sight of my foot offend you?"

"If not the sight, the smell surely will!" Claire teased. "Mayhap you should have a bath, too, Simon."

"I am *speaking* to Mouse."

"Your foot does not offend," Mouse said.

"I did not think so. Yet, once I suffered a wound much worse than yours. It happened long before I came to these parts, when I was visiting the maharaja of India at his palace made of rubies and gold. Have you ever been to India, Mouse? No? Well, believe me, it is a strange and wonderful place. In the mountains lives a race of people called Pygmies, standing no taller than my knee. And any time of day or night you are apt to see elephants wandering the streets and monkeys playing in the trees."

"Elephants?" Mouse asked.

"You have never seen one? Elephants are tall as a hillock, gray as winter rain. Their noses are long, like the branch of a tree, and curved at the end. Their ears are flat and round as river stones."

"Elephants!" Claire scoffed. "Pygmies and gold palaces. I should be ashamed to fill this child's head with such nonsense."

But Simon went on. "I swear it, Mouse. India is a wondrous place, fairly bursting with tall mountains and deep, green rivers. It was just such a river that was the cause of my misfortune.

"One day I decided to go for a swim, for India is surely the hottest place in all the world. No sooner had I gone into the water than a crocodile latched on to my foot and would not let go. Just as I was thinking I would surely die, a passing fisherman fought off the murderous beast and brought me safely to shore. Half my foot was hanging down, as if suspended by a single thread. But the fisherman bound it up with salves and potions, and now I am completely healed, as you can see."

He pulled on his stocking and jammed his foot into his boot. "Cease your worries, little one. In time all will be well. Are you hungry?"

When there was nothing left of their repast but a pile

of greasy bones, Simon wiped his hands, tossed more wood onto the fire, and brought out his lute.

Claire patted the ground beside her. "Come sit here, Mouse, and I will braid your hair."

While Alice hummed a nameless tune and the stars came out, shining like new coins, Claire braided Mouse's hair and tied it with a length of ribbon taken from the sleeve of her cloak. Mouse studied the dear faces of her traveling companions. So this was what It was like to have a family.

Simon began a new song:

"On the road to London town, I met a maiden fair.
She wore a snow-white linen gown, and ribbons in her
*   hair.*
Her brown eyes shone like summer rain, oh, ne'er shall I
*   forget.*
Because she did not have a name, I called her Vi-o-let."

He is singing about me! Mouse thought happily.

Simon smiled at her across the flickering campfire. "What about it, Mouse? Would you like that name?"

"It is a pretty name, but I am more thorn than flower," she said ruefully.

"I cannot say I agree with you, but all right. Some brave name, then. Ronalda, perhaps. Or Georgette."

"I am not very brave, either," Mouse said.

"Pish and tosh! You are as brave as you decide to be. Anytime you need a bit of courage, do what I do."

"And what might that be?" Claire asked, amused.

"Why, I stand very tall, close my eyes, and say to myself, 'I am brave and strong.' It has never failed me yet."

Mouse looked doubtful. Simon said, "What shall we name you, then? A serious name, perhaps. Wilhelmina might suit you. Or Esmerelda or Henrietta."

"Oh, no! Not Henrietta!" Alice put in. "I have a pet goose by that name. She is a dear old thing but dumb as a stone. I should not like to see our little Mouse named Henrietta."

Simon sighed. "This task has proved more difficult than I thought. We shall leave it for another day." Opening his pouch, he took out his potions and knelt at Mouse's side. "Hold still, little one. Let me tend your wound."

When that was done, Claire stood up and held out her hand. "We must rest. Coming, Mouse?"

They passed the night by the side of the road. In the morning they ate the last of the bread and honey and bundled their belongings once more.

"Ah," Simon said as they turned down the sun-dappled road. "I feel like singing a morning song."

Walking between Alice and Claire, with the sun on

her face and the wind at her back, Mouse felt like singing too. She slipped her hands into theirs, and they continued on, just so, until they arrived some days later in York.

CHAPTER THREE

The Inn

To Mouse, who had never before ventured beyond the fields and forests at Dunston Manor, the city of York was a wonder. From the center of town, the streets led away in every direction, each of them lined with houses, shops, and inns all standing atop one another like piles of stones. It was market day, and the town was abustle with carts, oxen, horses, and more kinds of people than Mouse had ever known existed in the world. Nuns and priests, shopkeepers and farm folk, jugglers and stilt walkers mingled in the streets, their voices rising and falling like the drone of bees. Mouse let go of Claire's hand and ran ahead, turning this way and that, determined not to miss a single thing.

One street overflowed with wool merchants and candlemakers, the next with ironmongers and leather-workers, ribbon sellers and fortune-tellers. The air was thick with the smells of baking bread and horseflesh, goose droppings and cheese. And the din! People shouted. Carts rattled. A church bell tolled.

As the travelers pressed through the teeming crowd, Simon said, "Come along, Mouse. Soon it will be dark, and we must find beds for the night."

"If it please you, not yet," Mouse said. "Fenn says the fortune-teller can see your whole future in the blink of an eye. I want to visit one."

"Then you shall be a slave to want," Simon declared firmly. "We must hurry, for the inns will be full. I know an innkeeper not far from here. Perchance he will let us pass the night, if only in his stables."

When they came to a place where three streets met, Alice said, "Here is where I must leave you." Bending down, she pressed a single coin into Mouse's hand. "Take this, little one. For the devil dances in an empty pocket."

Mouse's eyes felt hot. "Stay with us."

"And leave poor Henrietta and the others to fend for themselves?" Alice smiled. "I must go, but mayhap you will visit me in Depford someday. Anyone in the village can tell you where I live. We shall have ale and raisin cakes, and you will tell me of all your great adventures. Promise you will come."

Mouse could only nod. Her throat ached with the effort of holding back her tears.

"Good fortune, dear Mouse," Alice said. "I do hope we will meet again."

Then she disappeared into the crowd.

Claire said, "Hurry, Mouse. Simon's patience grows thin. We must not tarry any longer."

Mouse tucked the coin into her tunic pocket and followed Claire and Simon to a square, gray building with two rows of grimy windows across the front. Beside the door hung a sign with a lion's head painted on it. From inside came a jumble of rattling plates, loud voices, and even louder laughter.

Lifting the door latch, Simon ushered them inside to a room filled with long wooden tables laden with platters of meat, bowls of pudding, tankards of ale. The smells of damp wool, old grease, and sweat made Mouse's nose twitch. Most of the guests seated at the tables were men in rough clothes, but at the end of one table, a well-dressed woman in a blue cloak and a plumed hat perched on her chair prim as a princess. She nodded to Mouse, and Mouse smiled back, glad that her tunic was still clean and her hair still in its neat braid.

One of the men looked up. A toothless smile spread across his broad face. "Simon Swann! They said ye were hanged for thieving!"

"Not true!" Simon said, his green eyes dancing. "As

you can see, I am quite alive and in the company of the most beautiful women in the realm. Where else would I bring them save the Lion's Head Inn?"

"Where else would you dare beg a room and a meal without a single coin in your pocket?"

Simon laughed. "Riches only increase want, my friend, so I make a point of being poor. But you are right. We have made a long journey. My companions need a goodly meal and a soft bed for the night. I myself will be quite content to sleep in the stables with the other lowly beasts."

The innkeeper stared at the weary travelers. Mouse thought of the coin in her pocket. Mayhap he would take it in payment for a bed for Claire, whose blue eyes seemed to grow sadder by the day. Accustomed to sleeping on the stone floor at Dunston Manor, Mouse cared little for her own comfort. A mound of sweet-smelling straw in the stable, with Simon close by to watch over her, seemed a fine idea.

But then Simon spoke. "I will sing for our supper and our beds. Three songs and a new poem, composed especially for the occasion."

"What occasion?" the innkeeper inquired, narrowing his eyes.

"It must be one saint's day or another. I will think of something, unless I fall asleep first."

"That has always been your trouble, Swann," the innkeeper said. "Irresponsible to a fault."

"He who is faultless must also be lifeless," Simon declared, grinning. "Four songs, then, if you would drive such a hard bargain."

When the innkeeper hesitated, Claire said wearily, "No matter. What is one more night beneath the open sky? It might be more pleasant than this wretched place."

"You must forgive Claire," Simon said. "Exhaustion brings out her ill temper."

"And what of this child?" The innkeeper peered into Mouse's face. "How did you get that wound, girl? Stealing chickens?"

Before Mouse could make an answer, Simon said, "She is no thief, but a hapless child who met with an accident on the road. She comes from a manor house some distance away and is merely on a short holiday."

"A holiday, you say? In those rags?" He bent so close, Mouse could smell his hot, oniony breath. "Harboring strangers by night is a dangerous business. I mean to know who sleeps beneath my roof."

"She comes from Dunston," Simon said quickly. "Five songs, and that is my final offer. Though if you ask politely enough, I might sing six."

The innkeeper grimaced as if he had swallowed sour

milk. Before he could reply, the door opened, and in came a young boy in rough boots and a dust-covered cloak. On a cord around his neck hung a slender silver flute.

"Will Gooding!" Simon cried, rushing to clasp the boy's hand. "I looked for you in Marlingford, but they said you had already gone."

"Something came up," the boy said, shaking the dust from his cloak.

"No matter. I am at this moment in the midst of bargaining for our keep. Mayhap you will favor this company with some songs of your own."

"I cannot stay," Will said, setting his leather pouch on the floor. "I only stopped for a drink of water and directions to the abbey. My uncle has arranged for me to study music there."

"You are giving up life on the road?" Simon asked. "I will sorely miss seeing you at the fairs."

The innkeeper turned to the newcomer. "It is too far to travel to the abbey this late. You may as well stay the night, Gooding. That is, if you can pay for it."

"I have a few coins left," the boy said pleasantly.

Simon turned to the innkeeper. "What of our bargain? Six songs in exchange for our supper and a night's lodging for my companions."

"Very well," the innkeeper said wearily. "But you

must be gone by the time the cock crows. Tomorrow the fair opens, and many customers there will be with coins aplenty."

"Done!" Simon agreed. "Let us eat first, and then the entertainment shall begin."

Bowls of soup and hunks of bread and cheese were brought for the travelers. Mouse ate until she could not swallow another bite. When Simon had eaten his fill, he wiped his mouth and took out his lute. The room grew quiet. Claire took a chair in the corner and drew Mouse onto her lap. While Simon sang, Claire hummed softly. The sound of it filled Mouse with such bittersweet longing, she feared her heart would break.

So this is what it is like to have a mother, she thought, winding her arms tightly around Claire's neck. Simon finished his first song, and the travelers clapped. Then Will Gooding brought out his flute and played a series of clear, sweet notes that seemed to dance in the air. Mouse struggled to stay awake, but the fire was warm, her belly was full, and she slept till the innkeeper at last took up his candle and led them along a narrow staircase to a sleeping room under the eaves. There, she burrowed into the warm straw mattress beside Claire.

Before dawn Claire woke her.

"Listen, Mouse," she whispered. "I have some news."

Mouse sat up on the straw mattress, rubbing her eyes. By the dim light of the sputtering candle, she saw that Claire was already dressed, her clothes brushed, her hair wound into a neat coil at the back of her neck.

"Remember the woman we saw last night?" Claire whispered. "The one in the blue cloak?"

Mouse nodded, feeling suddenly uneasy.

"Her name is Lady Ashby. She has agreed to take me into her household as companion to her children. Her home is far away, and we are leaving now."

"You cannot leave me!" Mouse cried. "Surely it was fate that brought us together, and Fenn says we must never tempt fate. If you go, something horrid is sure to happen."

"You must not believe everything you hear," Claire said quietly. "In time I am sure we will both find our places in the world." She smoothed Mouse's tangled hair. "Dear child, ever since I learned the truth about the man I loved, I confess there have been moments when I wondered about the very existence of our Lord. But do you not see? That he should have placed me here at the same moment as Lady Ashby, why, it truly is a miracle. If you wish to believe in fate, believe it has brought Lady Ashby to me."

Mouse swallowed hard.

"Simon will look after you," Claire said. "Despite his roguish tongue, he has a good heart."

Mouse grasped Claire's hand. "If it please you, ask the lady if I may come too. I will not be a bit of trouble. I can earn my keep."

"If only you *could* come with me," Claire said. "But I have no influence with the lady. I had to beg to be taken on myself. I dare not ask a favor so soon." Tucking the thin blanket around Mouse's shoulders, she said, "Go back to sleep and try not to worry. The morrow will take care of itself." She kissed Mouse's forehead. "God keep you, little one."

Then she was gone.

Huddled beneath the scratchy blanket, Mouse stared into the darkness, too miserable to sleep. A short while later, when the *clop-clop* of horses' hooves sounded on the cobblestones, she ran to the window and peered out.

Morning was on its way. The stars had faded. A thin line of gray painted the black rooftops. A coach turned through the arched gate, and in the carriage window Mouse caught a glimpse of Claire's yellow hair and Lady Ashby's plumed hat before the coach disappeared into the mist.

"I will not cry," Mouse said in a wobbly voice. "I am brave and strong."

Then the cock announced the new day. Mouse

washed her face and smoothed her hair. Her fingers closed over Alice's coin. Mayhap Simon would take it in exchange for seeing her safely to London. There, she was certain to make her own way, if only in the scullery of some fine house.

Tiptoeing down the darkened staircase, she eased open the door and hurried across the yard, scattering the geese in her path. She slipped inside the dim, hushed stable. A horse bobbed his head, nickered and danced sideways in his stall.

"Simon?"

Hearing no answer, Mouse crept farther into the shadows and called more loudly, "Simon?"

Then a stableboy swung wide the door. In the pale light of morning, Mouse saw the hollowed-out place where Simon had passed the night. But he had vanished.

Lute, leather pouch, and all.

CHAPTER FOUR

The Puppeteer

"There ye be!" the innkeeper said, striding into the stable. "At least ye kept your end of the bargain. Where is Swann?"

"Gone," Mouse muttered sadly. "And Claire, too."

The innkeeper snickered. "Gone off together, no doubt. Well, good riddance. Swann is a charmer, true enough, but no more dependable than the weather. If ye ask me, ye are well rid of such a companion. Mayhap ye will find a more reliable one on the journey home."

Mouse said nothing. Now that she had tasted life on the road, she was more determined than ever not to return to Cook and his cruel ways. But with no one to guide her, she felt adrift in the world and jumpy as a flea.

The innkeeper clapped his hands, a sharp, unfriendly sound in the still morning. "Away with ye now."

"If it be not too much trouble," Mouse began, "a bit of bread and meat for my journey?"

"Swann bargained for supper and a bed. Nothing more."

"I will work for it," Mouse said. "I can peel onions, knead bread, sweep the floor, and stir the pots as well as anyone."

"That may be, but that face of yours would slay the devil himself. There is no work here for ragtags and crones."

Mouse touched the long, crusty scab on her cheek. It had begun to heal, and, as Simon had predicted, she rarely thought of it. Now the innkeeper's words reminded her of just how unpleasant she must look.

"Well, off ye go," he said, shooing her out the door.

Mouse left the inn, her thoughts a-jumble. She had considered the travelers her first true friends. More than friends. Almost like a real family. But Simon had left her without so much as a by-your-leave. Alice and Claire were far away. Mayhap she never would see them again. She had not realized friendship meant sorrow as well as joy.

She reached the center of town. The fair was under way, and it was such a lively celebration that Mouse almost forgot her troubles. The streets overflowed with minstrels playing tambourines and flutes, with jugglers and magicians, and peddlers selling live ducks, candles, and wheels of cheese. In a meadow near the end of the road, a spirited horse auction was taking place. As the animals came up for sale, the bidders shouted and waved their arms. Mouse watched as a man bought a sleek brown mare and led the animal away. Then something even more exciting caught her eye.

Beyond the auction yard, beneath a fluttering yellow banner, stood a wagon painted with splashes of bright green, crimson, and blue. One side was open to reveal a small stage, and there a crowd had gathered to watch two wooden figures singing and dancing. The little wooden dolls moved as effortlessly as if they were truly human. Behind the stage stood an open trunk brimming with more puppets. Mouse stared at them, at the tangle of wires and strings and rainbow-colored costumes, the jumble of arms and legs and brightly painted faces spilling out.

That is where the puppets live, she thought. Remembering the gloomy, airless corner at Dunston Manor where she had dreamed she might one day be part of the wider world, she imagined the puppets, too, were waiting in the dark of their trunk for something wondrous to happen. She edged closer. "You are like me," she whispered.

Above the buzz of the horse auction and the din of street peddlers hawking their wares, Mouse heard the crowd laughing at the puppets' antics. The sound of it touched something deep inside her. As if drawn by a sorcerer's spell, she pushed her way through the onlookers till she was standing at the very edge of the stage.

A wooden jester in a gold and purple cape floated across the stage. Mouse marveled at the way his arms moved in time to his piping song. Then a second jester appeared, bowed low, and began to dance. Now Mouse could see the fine wires running through the puppets' heads and the strings that connected their arms and legs. It was the strings, she saw, that enabled the figures to turn their heads, lift a shoulder, run, jump, dance.

The jesters' song ended, and the puppets disappeared behind a crimson curtain. From behind the stage came a series of bumps and rustlings, mutterings and shufflings. Then a bearded puppet dressed in a loose-fitting robe tied at the waist with a brown velvet cord came onto the stage.

From the left side of the stage, a puff of smoke appeared, and a voice said, "Noah!"

The puppet knelt on the stage and folded his hands.

"You shall build an ark," came the voice again.

A parade of animal puppets crossed the stage two by two. First came a pair of fierce-looking beasts Mouse imagined were tigers, then two large gray figures with noses like tree trunks and round flat ears.

"Elephants!" Mouse shouted.

A fishwife standing beside her poked her in the ribs. "Quiet, girl!"

Next came horses, cows, and goats.

I know this story, Mouse thought. *It is the one about the great flood and the rainbow the visiting priest read at Dunston last year.*

The puppet Noah lifted his arms. A shower of water spilled onto the ground in front of the stage. Everyone clapped as a rainbow drifted down, as if from heaven.

Mouse stood there wonderstruck, as close to perfect happiness as she had ever been in her short life. It was as if a heavy veil suddenly had been lifted from her eyes, giving her a glimpse of a brighter world she had not even known existed. Right then she understood that her future lay not in some dank scullery in London, but with these puppets who moved by some magic she did not yet understand. Somehow, she must learn their secrets. Somehow, she and the puppets must belong to each other.

When the show ended, she waited until the crowd had gone. Then she walked boldly to the wagon and rapped on the shuttered window.

"Go away!" came a voice from inside.

"If you please, I must talk to you."

"Leave me be!"

Again, Mouse rapped on the shutter.

Suddenly it flew open, and a head appeared. "What?"

Mouse stared. The puppeteer wore a turban and a hooded crimson cloak that hid everything but a black patch covering one eye. "I—I," she stammered. "The puppets. They are wondrous."

"I quite agree. Good day."

"Wait!" Mouse cried, so desperately full of love for the puppets that she could barely contain herself. Words jumped and bumped together inside her head and spilled out too fast. "How do the puppets dance? Is it magic? Will you teach me?"

The puppeteer fixed her with one bright blue eye. "Teach you? What an absurd notion."

The shutter slammed tight. If only Mouse could have described all the feelings churning inside her when she had watched the puppets dance, mayhap she could have convinced the puppeteer to teach her what she longed to learn. But now her chance was lost. Cook was right, she thought as she turned away, stepping carefully around the horse manure and goose droppings littering the road. She was naught but an addlebrained clod. Her throat ached painfully, but tears were useless. She wandered aimlessly among the peddlers and musicians till she came at last to the fortune-teller's cart.

"Tell yer fortune, girl?" asked the woman with a broken-toothed smile.

Though in desperate need of goodly advice, Mouse dared not squander her only coin. She shook her head, but the fortune-teller's meaty hand closed over her arm. "Well, then, would yer mind standing here and pretending for a while? I have been here since the cock's first crow, and not a single person has stopped to ask a question. Never have I met a less curious lot of folk."

Mouse tried to free herself, but the woman held her fast. "I will not harm ye, girl. In town for the fair?"

Mouse hesitated, then nodded.

"What are ye selling, then? Meat pies? Wool? Goats?"

"I have nothing to sell."

The fortune-teller shifted in her chair, and Mouse yanked her arm free.

"Come now," the woman said, picking up a dog-eared stack of odd-looking cards. "I will not charge ye for pretending. Tell me, in what month were ye born?"

"I do not know."

"Ah. So that is how it is. The cards will not help us, then. Spit into this cup."

Too curious to refuse such a strange request, Mouse spat, then watched as the fortune-teller slowly stirred the spittle with one long, broken fingernail, all the while muttering to herself.

"What?" Mouse cried when she could stand the suspense no longer.

The fortune-teller's dark gaze flitted from the cup to Mouse and back again. "For you I see a long journey, a great sorrow, and a dream fulfilled."

Just then a goat boy hurtled past, jostling Mouse so hard that she nearly fell. But the fortune-teller seemed not to notice. She clasped Mouse's hands and peered intently into her face. "Remember this: Some dreams are won by means of money spent, and some by tricks, and some by kindness lent."

While Mouse was pondering these words, the goat boy returned. With a slight nod to the fortune-teller, he walked on. Abruptly, the woman dropped Mouse's hands. "Enough pretending. The rain is starting. No customers today, I trow. Thanks be for yer help, girl. May good fortune be yer companion."

Mouse hadn't noticed the sun disappearing behind the spreading clouds, but now the sky darkened and a cold rain pelted her face as she ran through the streets. Finding herself once again at the Lion's Head Inn, she hurried across the courtyard and slipped into the stable.

After the clamor of the fair, the stable seemed eerily quiet. Dust motes swirled in the gray light coming through the cracks in the walls. The air was heavy with the smell of hay and horses. Mouse's ears rang in the silence.

Burrowing into the fresh straw, she thought about the fortune-teller's words. *Some dreams are won by means of money spent.* And a plan formed inside her head. She would pay to learn the puppeteer's secrets. On the morrow she would strike a bargain and soon she would possess the magic that made the puppets dance. Filled with determination, she reached inside her pocket for the coin that held the key to her future.

It was gone.

Mouse leapt to her feet and dug frantically through the mounds of straw on the floor, then yanked open the stable door and ran into the rain-slicked road. Mayhap her coin had lodged itself between the cobblestones or fallen into the gutter or rolled beneath some wool merchant's cart. She looked and looked, retracing her steps all the way to the meadow and back again, but plainly, her coin was lost. There was nothing to do but return to the stable.

"I will not cry," she told the dappled gray horse that watched her from his stall. "I am brave and strong."

But the words rang hollow in her ears. She slumped onto the hay, miserable and defeated.

The stable door opened, but Mouse didn't stir till a hand touched her shoulder. She looked into the calm gray eyes of the stableboy.

"You!" he exclaimed. "I thought you would be on your way home by now."

"I have neither home nor hope nor a single coin for bread."

He seemed willing to listen, so Mouse told him about the fortune-teller and the goat boy who had jostled her so roughly while she pretended to have her fortune told. She told him about her futile search for her lost coin. To her surprise, the stableboy laughed.

"That old swine! She and the goat boy are a team, I wager. While you were listening to her nonsense, the boy shoved you and stole your coin. It is a trick older than time itself, one that Swann knows well, no doubt."

The mention of Simon brought Mouse perilously close to tears. Despite his kindness on the journey to York, in the end she had mattered not at all.

The stableboy said, "If the master finds you here, he will flog us both. I can bring you some bread and cheese, and you may pass this night here. But you must go on the morrow."

He hurried out and presently returned with a crust of bread, a hunk of moldy cheese, and a wrinkled apple. Wordlessly, he dropped the food onto the hay and pulled the door firmly shut behind him. Mouse ate a bit of everything and saved the rest. She nestled into the hay. *Some dreams are won by kindness lent.*

What kindness could she perform that would change

the puppeteer's mind? She thought and thought, but it was a question without an answer.

And some by tricks. She hated tricks, but Simon had tricked her. And the fortune-teller and the goat boy. As she lay there, listening to the snuffling of the horses and the *drip-drip* of rain on the cobblestones, it seemed the only way to realize her dream was to trick the puppeteer into teaching her what she must learn.

Mouse slept little that night, for her mind was busy with a new plan. Even before the cock announced the new day, she rose, tucked her food inside her tunic, and pushed open the stable door.

The city was asleep. Deep shadows lay across the deserted streets. Here and there, the dim glow of a single candle illuminated the darkness. A dog barked in the distance. Mouse set off toward the meadow where the puppeteer's wagon stood, her mouth dry as sand. Her daring plan, which had seemed so easy when she was safe inside the stable, now seemed fraught with danger.

Suppose the puppeteer should suddenly emerge from the shuttered wagon and find her there? Suppose someone watching from a darkened window shouted an alarm?

"I am brave and strong," she whispered to an owl that rose, fluttering, from a treetop. Then she reached the wagon.

The puppeteer's horse nickered softly. Mouse gave him a bit of her apple, then hoisted herself onto the flat roof of the wagon. It was cold and slick with rain, but she lay completely still, watching the first light of the new morn seep into the sky.

Soon the turbaned puppeteer, dressed in a shapeless garment of faded gray wool, came out and made a cook fire. The smells of cooking meat and sweet onions wafted up. Mouse's empty stomach growled, and she reached for her bread. She chewed it slowly while the puppeteer finished eating, doused the campfire, caught the horse, and hitched the wagon.

By the time the sun had climbed above the trees, the rooftops of York were only a dark blur on the horizon and Mouse was sitting atop the puppeteer's wagon, munching the last of her apple as they rolled through the countryside.

CHAPTER FIVE

Mouse Is Discovered

Toward sunset they came to the edge of a small village, where a jumble of barns and gray, thatched-roof cottages sat close to the road. From her perch on the wagon's roof, Mouse watched a ribbon of gray smoke drift across the road and into the churchyard. There, a noisy band of children and dogs, goats and geese tumbled about in the fading light.

By the time the puppeteer halted the wagon in a nearby wood, Mouse longed for something to eat, a privy, and a drink of cool water. After the horse was unhitched, Mouse dropped noiselessly to the ground and hid in the trees. She squatted to relieve herself, and set off in search of water. She drank from a sluggish stream that meandered through the trees, then returned cautiously to the wagon.

The puppeteer was bent low over a cook fire, tending a pot of soup. Mouse's belly rumbled and her backside was sore from the bumpy wagon ride, but she dared not show herself and reveal her plan. Food was what she needed first. Then she would be ready.

The puppeteer ate quickly, then disappeared inside the wagon, leaving the pot bubbling on the fire. Mouse stole into the clearing, took out the last of her bread, and dipped it into the pot.

"Who goes there?" The cloaked figure rushed from the wagon, wielding a silver-handled sword.

Mouse backed away, wiping the soup from her chin. "I meant no harm."

Slowly, the puppeteer lowered the sword and peered intently into the gathering gloom. "By my troth! It cannot be and yet it is! The pest from York come to bedevil me again."

"I rode atop your wagon," Mouse confessed. "I want to be a puppeteer."

"Of course you do. Everyone does. But it is not an easy thing to learn."

"I learned to be a scullery maid," Mouse said with more boldness than she felt. "I can learn to make the puppets dance."

"Making soup and baking bread? Where is the skill in that?"

"It is not as easy as you think," Mouse declared. "Too much salt ruins the loaf. Too many turnips make a bitter soup."

"I suppose that is so," the puppeteer allowed.

"If it please you, I must learn all there is to know."

"Why?" The one blue eye bore into hers.

"Because the world is too full of tears."

"True enough," the puppeteer said thoughtfully, setting aside the sword. "Still, my work is an art, a calling some might say, learned through years of practice. Besides, it is hardly a suitable occupation for a girl. Your mother will not approve."

"I have neither mother nor father. No one at all."

"Ah. Mayhap it is not my knowledge you seek after all, but merely a roof over your head and food for your groaning belly."

"I could work in a scullery if that is all I wanted."

"An excellent plan! Mayhap some mistress in this very village is in need of a servant girl. Life on the road is not as easy or as exciting as you imagine. You would tire of it soon enough."

"I will do anything for a chance to be a puppeteer," Mouse said desperately. "It is my dearest wish in all the world." Then she took a deep breath and put her plan into action. "And you are in dire need of an assistant."

"Begging your pardon?"

"Yestermorn, when the jester's song ended, you took so long behind the curtain that I thought the crowd would leave before the show went on."

"Crowds never walk away from my shows."

Mouse continued. "And when Noah's rainbow came down, it came down crooked as a shepherd's staff."

"Crooked? It most certainly was not!"

"It was. You need a helper, and you will never find a better one than me."

Darkness had fallen. The puppeteer rose and tossed more twigs onto the dying fire. "You are not the first to beg the secrets of my art. In every village there is always one who thinks he can learn it. It grows quite tiresome."

"I am not like the others."

"No? Last year a boy from Reedham badgered me for a fortnight, till I agreed to take him on. After three days he discovered the life of a vagabond was not so glorious as he had imagined. So he ran away with a milkmaid from Dover without so much as a by-your-leave. You are no different. The first time some half-witted goat boy smiles in your direction, you will be gone. I am done with wasting time on starry-eyed dreamers."

"I will work for my lessons," Mouse said. "And I will not run away with a goat boy. I can tend your horse, make the fire, cook your supper, anything at all, if only you will show me how to make the puppets dance."

"What is your name, girl?"

"I am called Mouse."

"Ha! A girl named for a rodent. Quite unfortunate. And you have no mother or father, you say?"

"No. No one at all." Mouse held her breath. The fire crackled. An owl hooted.

Finally the puppeteer said, "I know what it is like to be alone in the world. And I suppose I cannot leave you here, though that is what you deserve."

Deep inside, Mouse felt a fluttering like the beat of a moth's wings, but mayhap it was hope. A look of delight spread across her thin face.

The puppeteer held up one hand. "We will try it for a fortnight, till we reach the fair in Marlingford. If you last that long! By then we shall know whether you are meant to be a puppeteer."

"I am!" Mouse cried. "I can feel it in my fingers when I look at them. I love the puppets, and they will love me, too. We are of one heart."

"You are an odd creature," the puppeteer said. "Mind you, I will not pay a single farthing for all your fetching and cooking and fire making. You will do exactly as I tell you. You must not touch anything without my leave. You will sleep in the back of the wagon beside the puppets' trunk, which you will find most uncomfortable. Though something tells me that is where you most desire to be."

Mouse could not stop smiling.

"Be warned," the puppeteer said. "If you are once late, I will leave you behind without a moment's regret."

"I will not be late," Mouse promised. "When may we begin my lessons? Mayhap we will start now."

"We shall begin on the morrow, and we shall begin at the beginning."

"I shall be ready at the cock's first crow," Mouse announced, fairly bursting with joy.

"And I shall be ready at noon."

So saying, the puppeteer retrieved the sword, opened the door to the wagon, and disappeared inside.

CHAPTER SIX

Mouse Discovers a Secret

For a long time after the puppeteer retired for the night, Mouse waited in the clearing beside the dying fire, afraid to seem too eager to claim her place inside. But at last, when the fire collapsed onto itself with a soft sigh, she rose and went in.

When her eyes adjusted to the dim light, she saw that the wagon was not as large as she had thought. On either side of the door were pegs that held the puppeteer's cloaks, and shelves lined with pots, tins, and brushes, all held in place by leather straps. On the opposite wall was a curtain. Mouse crept across the floor and lifted it, but it was too dark to see anything save a hinged door she thought must be the opening to the stage.

A sliver of pale moonlight illuminated the narrow mattress where the puppeteer slept beneath the shuttered window and cast a soft glow on the polished wood of the trunk at the back of the wagon. Mouse slid her fingers across its smooth surface before curling herself into a ball on the floor. On the morrow she would make the puppets dance. Which would she choose? The jester? The knight? The gray-bearded Noah or one of his animals? She wished she could tell Simon about the elephant puppet and the play she had seen in York.

Mouse was still thinking about it the next day when at last noon approached and the puppeteer summoned her from the stream, where Mouse had been washing linen. She spread the last of it on a bush to dry and hurried to the wagon.

"Make haste, girl," the puppeteer said. "I have too much to do to waste time with lessons that will surely come to naught."

Mouse dried her hands on her tunic. "If it please you, I have decided to begin with the knight. He is the finest puppet I have ever seen."

"Faint praise, coming from someone with so little experience in such matters," the puppeteer said wryly.

"What dance will I learn first?" Mouse asked.

"Did I not tell you we would begin at the beginning?" The puppeteer opened the trunk and laid the puppets on the grass. "First you will learn how they are made and how to care for them. There will be no dancing today."

Mouse opened her mouth to protest, then closed it again. She folded her hands and waited.

"They are carved from the wood of the ash tree, which makes them very heavy, but ash lasts much longer than birch or pine," the puppeteer began. "Their limbs are connected by means of strings, as you can see, the heads by these wires that are anchored in the bodies themselves. Their faces are painted and must be kept well away from sun and rain, lest they crack and peel."

"I will keep them safe," Mouse promised. "They are the most wondrous things in all the world."

The puppeteer's demeanor seemed to soften. "Quite so. The knight is called Sir Alfred. Next to him is Princess Bridget. She is very beautiful, but I am afraid she is not as kindhearted as one might wish. More than once she has broken poor Alfred's heart, though he is much too brave to show it."

Mouse looked into the puppet's brown eyes. Though he was made of wood and paint, bits of wire and cloth, it seemed she sensed the quiet, steady beating of his noble heart.

"Here are the two jesters you saw in York," the puppeteer continued. "They are impossibly mischievous but the best at warming up an unfriendly crowd. They are quite old and must be handled with the greatest of care."

"I will be careful."

"Next to the jesters is Noah. His beard comes off so he can play the part of a knight. The one in black with the cracked arm is the sorcerer, of course. And there is the dragon, who is not as fierce as he looks, but you need not tell him I said so, for he is quick to take offense. The rest are the animals for Noah's ark."

From a box filled with blocks of wood and horsehair brushes, with paint pots, metal blades, and a handful of sharp knives, the puppeteer chose a small-bladed knife and a block of wood and handed them to Mouse. "The sorcerer needs a new arm. You may as well learn to carve one."

They sat on the damp ground, and the puppeteer showed Mouse how to measure the length of the sorcerer's arm and how to trace its shape on the wood with the tip of the knife blade. The wood felt heavy in Mouse's hands, but she learned to cut it away in small strips, till the outline of the arm at last emerged and a pile of pale shavings curled about her feet.

"A bit crude, but not bad for your first try," the puppeteer said when Mouse had finished. "Mayhap carving a puppet's arm is not so different from peeling turnips after all."

"Will you show me how to wire it on?" Mouse asked eagerly.

"Oh, it must be much smoother than that, else our sorcerer will complain. Leave it for now and help me with Bridget's new gown. Her old one is faded, and she is quite insistent upon a new one before our next show."

Mouse stole a glance at the haughty, blue-eyed princess puppet lying in the shade of the wagon. *Make haste,* she seemed to say. *Do you not know better than to keep a princess waiting?*

The puppeteer handed Mouse a tiny gown of bright green silk and a pouch filled with white beads. "Sew these beads on to the skirt. They will look like pearls."

Mouse tried, but the silk was slippery and the beads were so small, she could not grasp them. The needle pricked her fingers, drawing droplets of blood, till at last the puppeteer said, "Enough for now. Help me put the puppets away, then make us something to eat."

They gathered the puppets and laid them carefully in the trunk. "Take care not to tangle the wires, Mouse," the puppeteer warned. "They are easily broken and the devil to repair."

Then, taking a series of tin boxes from the shelf inside the wagon, the puppeteer went on. "Here you will find barley and herbs for making soup. There is bread I bought in York and a bit of cheese. I do not suppose you know how to set a snare."

"I can learn," Mouse said.

The puppeteer led Mouse to a place along the stream where the day before the snare had been set, and showed Mouse how to set the stick and conceal the trap with leaves and brambles. They removed the hare caught inside and gathered wild onions growing beside the stream.

When they returned to the wagon, Mouse skinned the hare and set the soup pot to bubbling. The puppeteer took up Princess Bridget's green gown once more. "Mayhap there is time to finish this before nightfall. Go see if the wash has dried and bring it back, lest we forget it on the morrow."

Mouse hurriedly stirred the pot, then gathered the freshly washed linens and took them inside the wagon. She noticed a bit of Sir Alfred's cloak sticking out of the trunk and opened the lid to tuck it back inside.

It seemed Sir Alfred smiled at her. She looked into his kind brown eyes, and before she knew quite what was happening, she lifted him and held him tightly to her chest. "Did you see what I learned today?" she whispered. "Now I know how to carve an arm and set a snare and sew a costume."

All that in a single day? Mouse could not have been more certain of him had he actually spoken aloud.

"All right. Mayhap I have not yet mastered the needle and thread, but I will."

"Mouse?" the puppeteer called, banging on the door.

Mouse jumped. Sir Alfred slipped from her grasp and tumbled onto the floor with a sound like the click of crickets in the grass. The wire connecting his head to his body sprang loose and dangled crazily over his shoulder.

Mouse's fingers trembled as she tried to poke the wire back into place. It was too short. She stuffed Sir Alfred into the trunk and jammed the lid shut just as the puppeteer threw open the door.

"What keeps you, girl?"

"I was folding the linens, just as you asked." Mouse's mouth felt dry as dirt.

"Be quick about it, then. The soup is boiling over."

Mouse hastened outside to slice the bread and ladle the soup into their bowls. It smelled wonderfully of the fresh meat and wild onions, but with every bite, her stomach clenched as if she were swallowing dirty pond water. What would the puppeteer do when he discovered what she had done?

She swallowed a spoonful of soup and took a deep breath. Mayhap Sir Alfred's wire was not broken after all, but merely tangled. Mayhap it would easily be put to rights. It might have come loose when the wagon hit a rut and they had simply not noticed.

"Mouse?" the puppeteer said.

"What?"

"Have you not heard a single word I said?"

"Forgive me. I was not listening."

"So I noticed. What ails you, girl? An aching head? An unquiet stomach? Mayhap you have decided the life of a puppeteer is not for you after all."

"Oh, no!" Mouse cried. "It is all I want in the world."

"Then stop your dreaming. In Marlingford we must buy food and notions, for it is a long way from there to Reedham."

"I cannot help it. I am full of dreams."

"Well, put this list inside your head, if there be room in there amongst all your dreams. Candles. Soap. Flour. Cheese. A pack of needles and a green ribbon to finish Bridget's gown. A pot of glue."

Mouse struggled to remember it all, but it was hard to concentrate. She had heard the priest once tell Cook confession was good for the soul, but she dared not confess her mistake to the puppeteer.

"Some woolen cloth," the puppeteer continued, rising to poke the fire once more. "Apples. Goose fat. Salt. Good night, Mouse."

As she had done on the previous night, Mouse waited by the fire till all was quiet inside the wagon. Then she crept inside and lay down on her blanket beside the trunk.

"What shall I do, Sir Alfred?" she whispered. "I am in an awful mess."

Speak not aloud your fears and sorrows, but whisper them to the wind and go forth singing.

Despite her worry, sleep finally came. When Mouse awoke the next day, gray light was leaking through the cracks around the windows and the puppeteer was outside making the fire.

"Whisper to the wind and go forth singing," Mouse said to herself. She washed her face and went outside, humming one of Simon's tunes under her breath. The puppeteer, lost in the folds of a red cloak, was bent low over the fire.

"There you are, Mouse. And in a pleasant mood, I see. I thought you meant to sleep all day."

"I will set the snare," Mouse offered quickly. "Or mayhap we shall have fish. I saw one in the stream yestermorn."

"There is no time for snares or fish," the puppeteer said, glancing skyward. "A storm draws nigh, and we must be away. Some toasted bread and a bit of cheese will do us for now."

They ate hurriedly, without talking. Then Mouse said, "Shall I catch the horse?"

"Yes. Then gather some dry twigs for our kindling basket. Soon you will learn how welcome a goodly fire can feel at the end of a wet day."

The horse had wandered nearer the stream and stood

placidly cropping the new grass. Mouse led him up the rise to the wagon and tethered him there while she went to look for kindling. When she had gathered an armload of twigs, she returned to the wagon.

Next to the fire stood the puppeteer holding Sir Alfred. A wave of foreboding passed over Mouse as she clutched the firewood tightly to her chest. The air around her seemed to crackle, as if the approaching storm had already begun.

"I meant no harm," Mouse began, fighting her tears. "You startled me, and he fell. I tried to put the wire back, but it is too short."

"Of course it is too short, you addle brain! You have broken it in two. Did I not tell you to take care?"

"I should not have disobeyed you," Mouse said, cowering like a dog awaiting a blow. "Forgive me."

"I suppose it is my own fault for taking pity on the likes of you," the puppeteer fumed. "I should have known one cannot make a silk purse from a sow's ear, nor a puppeteer from an ignorant, willful girl."

Then the puppeteer wheeled around and disappeared into the wagon.

Before Mouse could finish loading the firewood onto the back of the wagon, the door opened again and she heard the jingle of harness as the horse was hitched. Cupping her hands to the window, she peered inside. Sir Alfred sat atop the trunk, his head falling onto his chest.

"It is true," Mouse told him. "I am naught but an addlebrained clod."

A part of her felt foolish, pouring her heart out to a figure made only of wood, yet somehow, it seemed Sir Alfred was listening. Somehow, it seemed he understood.

The puppeteer climbed onto the wagon, picked up the reins, and said coldly, "Move out of my way."

"I pray you, you cannot leave me here!" Mouse cried.

"I can and I will."

"But what shall I do?"

"That is none of my concern."

The wagon began to move, slowly at first, then it gathered speed as it rolled down the hill. A sudden clap of thunder echoed through the trees.

"Wait!" Mouse raced across the clearing. But the wagon, its yellow banner fluttering in the wind, rounded a bend in the road and disappeared.

"I will not cry," she said to the darkening sky. "I am brave and strong." Now she needed Simon's words more than ever.

She dropped onto the low fence beside the road, shivering as the storm blew in and the morning's feeble heat ebbed out of the stone. Above her the black tree limbs knocked together in the wind.

Soon the soaking rain rushed in, but she was too discouraged to care.

Later, she could not have said whether the storm lasted a minute or an hour; she merely waited numbly for it to pass.

When the rain slackened, she stood up, shivering, and set off down the road. As the day lengthened without a single sighting of either man or beast, it seemed she was the last person alive, alone in an empty world. *All is lost,* her footsteps seemed to say. *All is lost.*

A future without the puppets was too bleak to contemplate, so Mouse forced herself to think of other things. The smell of Fenn's bread baking in the hearth. The recipe for venison stew. The proper way to set a snare. Anything to keep from worrying about what would happen to her now. As evening approached, she looked for a barn, a shed, an abandoned cart where she could pass the night. Mayhap around the next bend in the road was a house where some kindhearted farmwife would give her a bed for the night in exchange for her help in the kitchen. Then she would think of what to do next.

On and on she walked, till the last gray light faded from the sky, but still there appeared no farmhouse, no barn or shed or cart, no weary plowman wending his way home. There was no sound save the rattling of the trees and the rustling of wind in the sedges beside the road. The mud sucked at Mouse's feet, slowing her steps. Her bones ached. Her stomach hurt. But there was nothing to do but keep going.

A faint, wavering light appeared through the distant trees. A farmhouse! Mouse began to run, imagining the warmth of the farmer's hearth and a bowl of savory soup for her groaning belly. Then from out of the darkness came the squeak and rattle of a wagon and a familiar voice.

"Is that you, girl?"

Mouse stopped short and peered into the gloom, afraid to trust her own senses.

"Well?" The puppeteer lifted a lantern and the dim light illuminated Mouse's weary, mud-streaked face. "Do you intend to stand there all night?"

"You came back!" Mouse clambered into the wagon.

"An astute observation. Now we must stop for the night, for I am too weary to go any farther."

"I passed a clearing not long before sunset. I do not think it too far out of our way."

The puppeteer tossed Mouse an oiled cloak and said gruffly, "Put this on. You are no good to me at all if you get sick."

Mouse wrapped herself in the warm cloak, too grateful for words. The horse stepped carefully along the rain-slicked road, the silence broken only by the jingle of his harness, the creaking of the wagon wheels, and the *clop-clop* of his hooves. At last the puppeteer said, "Never have I met a more vexing child. But I should not have left you alone in the wood."

"I should not have touched Sir Alfred without your leave," Mouse said.

"True enough. Are you hungry?"

"I have had naught to eat since morn. When we reach the clearing, I shall make us a supper."

"I will make a supper," the puppeteer said. "Tomorrow will be soon enough to take up your chores again."

"No, no, no," the puppeteer cried one morning many days later. "You must not jerk the strings, else he will seem more like a drunken lout than the hero of this tale."

With a weary sigh, Mouse lowered Sir Alfred onto the floor of the stage. Her muscles ached from the effort of holding the puppet aloft. Her fingers were sore from trying to keep the wires and strings from tangling. For days she had practiced the same simple movement, but her teacher was never satisfied.

"What ails you, Mouse?" the puppeteer asked, coming from behind the curtain.

"I am tired," Mouse said. "While you lay abed, I trapped a hare and mended three costumes. I have practiced with Sir Alfred for hours and hours, and yet you are not pleased."

"'Twas you who begged to work for me in exchange for my knowledge," the puppeteer reminded her. "But no matter. Another two days' journey will bring us to Marlingford. Mayhap you will find some mistress there who will take you in. For it is plain to me you will never be a puppeteer."

"I will!"

"No, you wish it were so, yet you do nothing but complain and we have not yet begun to work on the voices."

From the folds of the red cloak, the puppeteer produced a small, flat object with holes in the sides. "This is a *pivetta*, for making different voices when there are many puppets on the stage. It fits inside the mouth and you speak through it, like so."

The voice of Princess Bridget came through the *pivetta*, a high, whistling sound, like winter wind. Then the puppeteer lifted Sir Alfred and spoke in a lower voice that reminded Mouse of the croaking of frogs in the pond at Dunston Manor. Mouse frowned in concentration. Had Sir Alfred said, "merry May" or "marry me"? It was impossible to tell. Mouse paid close attention, though she did not quite understand the need for such a device, for already she had noticed the puppeteer's ability to change voices at will, speaking sometimes in a clear, musical voice like Claire's, and sometimes in deeper, richer tones like Simon's.

The puppeteer set Sir Alfred aside and removed the *pivetta*. "An imperfect thing, I will admit, but it is the best one can do when working alone. Now, begin again, and this time do not let your puppet stumble."

Mouse lifted Sir Alfred once more, and the practice went on until late in the day when at last the puppeteer said, "Enough."

Setting aside the heavy puppet, Mouse rubbed her aching arms and said, "I wish we were already in Marlingford, for I cannot wait to make the puppets dance. I hope we have a goodly crowd. Mayhap the king himself will come to our show."

The puppeteer laughed. "Not likely, Mouse. It is the ordinary folk who come to see our plays. Now kindle a fire and I will show you how to make a pudding, for I am bored beyond words with bread and soup."

So saying, the puppeteer deftly mixed the last of their flour with a splash of ale and a dash of spices, sweetened the mixture with honey, and set the bowl in a bucket of water suspended over the fire. "Let it steam while the meat is roasting. I am weary and would rest before we sup."

Mouse set the hare on the spit, thinking about the play they had practiced all afternoon and the song she had imagined for Princess Bridget. "He who seeks to win my hand, must be the bravest in the land," she sang as she set out the plates for their supper. Mouse nodded to herself. *A goodly song, if I do say so myself.* Would the puppeteer give her leave to try it? It would do no harm to ask. Leaving the hare sizzling on the spit, she opened the door to the wagon.

What she saw was so astonishing, she lost her balance and, with a loud yelp, toppled backward onto the wet grass.

In a trice the puppeteer was out of the wagon and standing over the incredulous Mouse. "So now you know."

"I—I," Mouse stammered. "Why did you not tell me?"

"That I am a woman?"

Impatiently, the puppeteer tossed the beribboned silver braid that had given away her secret. "It has naught to do with you." She bent down till their noses touched. "If you would continue as my apprentice, you will speak of this to no one."

"But why?"

"You must not ask questions. Say one word more and I will leave you in this wood faster than you can blink an eye. And this time I will not come back. Now, make haste and bring our supper."

Dazed, Mouse pulled the meat from the bone and set it on the plate. Hadn't the puppeteer said women were not meant to be puppeteers? That thought was an unsettling one, for the puppets were her family now and a life on the road the only one she wanted. She glanced at the puppeteer, sitting now with her knees drawn up before the fire. Why did the puppeteer travel in disguise? Had she broken an important law? Mouse's head was full of questions, but she feared asking them.

You are wise to be wary of strangers on the road, Alice had said, yet Mouse had begged to join the strange vagabond and her puppets with no thought for her own safety.

"What is it now, Mouse?" the puppeteer asked. In the light of the campfire, her expression was so guileless, Mouse was overcome with shame at harboring such unkind thoughts.

"I am wondering," Mouse said. "What name will I call you?"

The puppeteer frowned. "The night grows cold. Fetch more wood for the fire."

Mouse hurried to obey, nearly tripping over her own feet in the process.

"Watch how you go!" The puppeteer held out a steadying hand.

"I am jumpy as a flea. In two days' time I will make the puppets dance. And I have made a song for Princess Bridget. It goes like this—"

"*I* shall make the puppets dance," the puppeteer interrupted. "You are not yet ready."

Seeing the disappointment on Mouse's face, the puppeteer continued more gently, "Do not despair, Mouse. If the day dawns fair, the crowds will come, and there will be plenty of work for both of us. Tell me, is our pudding done yet?"

Mouse spooned the pudding into their bowls and, when the pot was empty, washed their dishes in the stream. Then they banked the fire and retired for the night. When the puppeteer was snoring softly, Mouse carefully lifted Sir Alfred from the trunk. "What secrets does she guard?" she whispered, holding him close. "Am I in danger?"

But Sir Alfred did not answer.

CHAPTER SEVEN

The Puppet Play

In Marlingford the wagon jostled along the rutted lanes, past stilt walkers and baxters with their loaves of fragrant bread, past musicians and candlemakers, and a tar-footed woman with a gaggle of hissing geese. As the wagon rolled along, Mouse peered at the goose woman, hoping it might be Alice. But of course it wasn't. Mouse wondered whether Claire had found her place in the world and what had become of Simon. Why had he pretended to be her friend, only to disappear like chimney smoke? She would ask Sir Alfred. Mayhap he would know the answer.

"Stop!" shouted a man in the crowd. "Stop, thief!"

A skinny boy and a woman in a purple cloak raced pell-mell in front of the puppeteer's wagon, shoving aside children and upending a baxter's cart in their haste to escape.

"I know them!" Mouse cried, tugging hard on the puppeteer's cloak. "It is the fortune-teller and the goat boy from York. The ones who stole my coin. Stop! I want to get it back."

"Sit down and be quiet," the puppeteer said fiercely. "You coin is long since spent, Mouse. It will do no good to raise a fuss now."

"Mayhap the sheriff will catch them," Mouse said, settling onto the seat again. "Mayhap he will put them in jail forever, with naught to eat but bread and water."

A brief smile lit the puppeteer's face. "A fate well deserved, I am sure."

When they reached the edge of town, the puppeteer halted the wagon. They unhitched the horse, then the puppeteer took out her money box and gave Mouse two coins and a scrap of green silk. "Take this to the ribbon seller and tell her the color must match exactly. These coins will buy enough to finish Bridget's new gown before the afternoon's play."

"What of the other things we need?" Though Mouse did not wish to question the puppeteer's judgment, it seemed foolish to buy ribbons when they had no bread. "What of flour and soap and candles?"

"Our purse is nearly empty, true enough, but after our play we shall have coins aplenty. Then we shall buy all we need for our journey to Reedham. Watch how you go, Mouse, and come back straightaway, for there is much to be done."

Mouse hurried along the road, past the wool merchant's carts, past the cheese sellers, past two stilt walkers entertaining a group of children, till she came to the ribbon seller's stall. While she waited her turn, she watched a jester dancing to a piping tune. The music reminded her of the puppets. If only she might have a part in this day's play!

"Begging your pardon," said a voice at her elbow, a man's voice with the scratch of metal in it. She looked up. Way up, for the man who had spoken was taller than anyone she had ever seen. He was dressed in black from head to toe. Thick black hair curled about his shoulders. Even his eyes were black. Around his neck dangled a silver medallion.

He smiled down at Mouse. "Did I not see you this morn, arriving aboard the puppeteer's wagon?"

"I am the puppeteer's apprentice," she said proudly. She handed her coins and the strip of green cloth to the ribbon seller.

"Indeed? And what is his name?"

Mouse blinked and looked about. What name would protect the puppeteer's identity? The picture on the sign outside the alehouse provided an answer. "He is called Lamb," she said quickly.

"Lamb, is it? Mayhap I shall come to see your play. What story will you tell?"

"Come and see for yourself."

The man laughed. "You are a clever one, to keep the customer guessing. Now I suppose I shall have to attend, to satisfy my curiosity."

The ribbon seller held two lengths of green ribbon against the scrap of silk. "Which will you have, girl?"

The man said, "Forgive me. I am keeping you from your errand. Good day."

He disappeared into the growing crowd. Mouse chose a length of ribbon and waited while the ribbon seller wrapped it in a bit of brown paper. Then she hurried back to the wagon.

"At last!" The puppeteer took the ribbon, and with a few quick stitches, expertly attached it to the bodice of Princess Bridget's gown. Mouse smoothed Bridget's yellow hair. With a soft cloth kept for the purpose, she polished the puppet's face till it shone. Though Mouse loved Sir Alfred best, she thought Bridget the most beautiful thing in the world.

"She is pleased with her new gown," Mouse said to the puppeteer. Then to Bridget: "Are you not?"

It is no more than I deserve, Bridget said. *But thank you for the ribbon all the same.*

"Hoist our banner, Mouse, then bring out the drum,"

the puppeteer said. "And do not forget our coin box. The time for our play draws nigh."

While Mouse attended to her chores, the puppeteer lifted Sir Alfred from the trunk and placed him on the stage. Today, he wore a white robe with a red cross on the front. Then came Princess Bridget in her new green gown, and the sorcerer with the new arm Mouse had carved for him.

Today's story of St. George and the dragon was one of Mouse's favorites. Sir Alfred, so handsome and brave, made a perfect St. George. When no one was looking, she planted a swift kiss on the puppet's cheek.

"Though I have but one good eye, I can plainly see what you are thinking, Mouse," the puppeteer said. "But this work is harder than it seems. Mayhap in another fortnight you will be ready for a small part. We shall see. For now, stand here and make ready to open the curtain. Be certain the smoke box is ready, then keep a sharp eye on our money box, lest some sticky-fingered thief helps himself to our hard-earned coins."

Mouse beat the drum, *rat-a-tat-tat*. Two goat boys in tattered breeches clambered over the stone fence to claim places near the stage.

Rat-a-tat-tat. Down the road came the ribbon seller. Close behind walked a goose woman trailing geese and a round-faced priest in a brown robe. *Rat-a-tat-tat.* Musicians and milkmaids, farmers and fishwives took their places and waited with expectant faces for the story to begin.

The puppeteer, her face shadowed by a hooded blue cloak, came out to greet them. "Welcome, one and all. As the feast day of St. George draws nigh, we present the story of his battle with the dragon, with a bit of romance and magic added to enliven the tale."

A sudden movement near the back of the crowd drew Mouse's attention. The tall man from the ribbon seller's stall caught her eye and doffed his black hat. Proud to have brought in a paying customer, Mouse waved to him. She turned to tell the puppeteer of her encounter with the man, but her mentor was busy with last-minute preparations.

"Ready, Mouse?" With a quick nod, the puppeteer took her place behind the curtain. Mouse pulled the cord, the curtain parted, and there sat Princess Bridget in her new costume. Working from her perch above the stage, the puppeteer inserted the *pivetta* into her mouth.

"Who calls here?" Bridget piped.

"It is George," came the answer in a deeper voice. The puppeteer moved Sir Alfred onto the stage. Applause rippled through the crowd as he knelt at the feet of the haughty princess.

Mouse readied the smoke box. She placed a glowing coal in the bottom of the metal box, added some small twigs she had soaked in water, and clamped the lid shut. Then she settled in to watch the puppets. So spellbinding were they that she soon forgot they were not real. Beneath the skilled hands of the puppeteer, they seemed every bit as alive as the farmers and shopkeepers, goatherds and serving girls standing awestruck at the foot of the stage.

"The one who wins my hand must first prove himself worthy," Bridget said.

It was time for the smoke box. Mouse opened the lid and released the swirling gray cloud the smoldering twigs had made. At that moment the sorcerer appeared and, with a wave of his newly carved arm, conjured the fiery dragon.

The crowd hissed at the fearsome creature, then clapped as Sir Alfred, playing the part of St. George, faced his foe.

Step by menacing step, the dragon stalked the knight. Sir Alfred raised his sword and began to parry and thrust. The dragon roared. Sir Alfred fell and lay still.

"Ohhh!" cried the crowd. Princess Bridget rose from her chair and rushed to the side of the fallen knight, her skirt billowing in the spring breeze like a green sail.

The dragon reared. Closer and closer he came to the knight and the princess.

Mouse saw that the priest standing closest to the stage was chewing his nails. The milkmaids hid their faces.

The crowd seemed to know what came next. They fell silent and craned their necks, intent upon the story unfolding in front of them. It was so miraculous that Mouse could no longer bear to be left out of it, despite the puppeteer's warnings. She seized Sir Alfred's strings and jerked him to his feet. His head fell heavily to one side. Mouse quickly released one string and pulled another one. Sir Alfred's leg crumpled. The crowd tittered.

The puppeteer's eye widened, and she gave a frantic shake of her head. Mouse yanked the strings again, and Sir Alfred lurched toward the dragon. The spell was broken; the crowd hissed and hooted.

"Whoever 'eard of a knight comin' back from the dead?" one of the goat boys jeered.

"He is not dead, ye addle brain! He is St. George. He will slay the dragon yet!"

"This play 'as got it all wrong!" someone yelled.

"Poor sod walks like he had too much ale, if ye ask me!"

Red-faced and stiff with shame, Mouse tried desperately to right her puppet, but Sir Alfred collapsed atop the dragon's back, a graceless tangle of arms and legs and fiercely bobbing head.

"Ach!" cried a fishwife. "Now he rides the dragon like a horse!"

Then a hail of raw eggs and rotten turnips pelted the stage. A turnip smashed into the dragon and rolled across the floor till it came to rest at Mouse's feet. Princess Bridget's new gown was stained yellow with broken eggs. The puppeteer jerked the cord, and the curtain closed. The jeering crowd moved away.

"Well?" the puppeteer demanded furiously. "What have you to say for yourself this time, Mouse?"

"I beg you, forgive me," Mouse said tearfully. "I meant to obey you, but the play was so wondrous, I forgot."

"You forgot. Mayhap you will remember this: Because of you we have not a single coin for food. What is worse, word will spread that we are but amateurs and the play worthless. I may as well hitch the wagon and move along. There will be nothing for me now."

Mouse stood in miserable silence, trying not to show the fear rising up in her at the thought of being abandoned yet again. But she knew it was what she deserved.

The puppeteer was a whirlwind, packing up the puppets, putting away the props. "By all the saints in heaven! Stupidity hangs upon you like a disease. You may as well go back from whence you came, for there is naught I can teach a girl like you."

"If you will give me another chance, I promise to obey."

"Another chance, Mouse? How many chances does one person deserve? Have I not already forgiven you for stealing aboard my wagon and for breaking Sir Alfred's wire? I have done my best to teach you what you wish to learn, but my words pass through your ears like water through a sieve."

"I know I am addlebrained and willful," Mouse said. "But there is naught I want in life except to be a puppeteer. And I dare not go back to Dunston now."

"That is your problem. Leave me now. I am tired, and my belly wants a good meal, though it may as well not, since we are without a single farthing and our cupboard is bare."

Mouse turned and ran, her thoughts racing faster than her feet. There was naught she could do now about the ruined play, but the puppeteer would not go hungry on her account. She crossed the road and turned down a narrow alley that ran behind the alehouse and toward the center of the village till she came to the courtyard of a fine house. Following her nose to the kitchen, she peered through the window.

The almoner had not yet arrived to remove the remains of the last meal; the table was laden with half-eaten loaves of bread, slabs of meat, a quince tart.

Mouse crept closer and pressed her ear to the door. All seemed quiet, so she slowly lifted the latch. It opened with a tiny *click* and the door swung wide.

As quick and quiet as her namesake, Mouse scooped all she could carry into her tunic and ran out, closing the door silently behind her. As she passed the alehouse, she heard heavy footsteps close behind her. "Zounds!" she muttered. Had the almoner spied her pilfering the kitchen after all? She darted into the darkened alley and hid in the shadows as the footsteps quickened, then halted abruptly.

Pressed tightly against the damp stone wall, Mouse held still. Whoever was following her was now so close she could hear his breathing. She wanted to scream, but fear closed her throat and stole her breath.

Suddenly the alehouse door opened. Three men stumbled out and set off together down the alley. Light spilled onto the silent, empty street.

Mouse leaned against the wall, waiting for her pulse to slow. Nothing stirred, save a cat slinking through the shadows. She peered into the darkness. Who would want to harm her? It had seemed real, but mayhap it was nothing more than a trick of her imagination. With another glance down the deserted alley, she hurried to the wagon.

The puppeteer was inside. Mouse hurriedly kindled a

fire, heated the meat, and toasted the bread. Then she knocked on the door. There was no answer, nothing but a muffled snuffling sound. Mouse ran to the window and peered in. On the trunk sat the puppeteer, holding fast to the sorcerer and weeping as if her heart would never mend. Mouse stared, trying to make sense of it. Had the sorcerer's arm broken again? Never had she seen the puppeteer in tears. She opened the door.

"What do you want now?" the puppeteer asked, hastily wiping her eye.

"I have brought your supper."

"A jest, Mouse, after all you have done to vex me?"

"I took it from a kitchen in the village. They will never miss it." Mouse perched on the edge of the trunk. "I thought it would be easy to make Sir Alfred slay the dragon, but you were right. I am not ready. Mayhap I am good for naught but skinning hares and peeling turnips, but when I talk to Sir Alfred, it seems—" She stopped, shamed at looking even more foolish in the puppeteer's eyes.

To her surprise, the puppeteer nodded, as if talking to puppets were the most natural thing in the world. "The sorcerer is the one who listens to all my troubles."

"You talk to them too?"

"Since I was a child. They are good listeners, are they not? When I feel afraid, I pretend the sorcerer has cast a spell to take away all my fears. And truth to tell, Mouse, we could use a bit of magic."

"Why are you afraid?" Mouse asked.

"It will do no good to dwell on it." The puppeteer set the sorcerer aside. "I hope you were not joking about my supper, for I am hollow all the way to my toes."

Mouse took the puppeteer's hand and led her outside. "See? There is bread and meat and a quince tart with only a single bite missing."

"I would not encourage you to become a thief, but since you have gone to so much trouble, I suppose I must eat it."

She sat upon her stool and broke off a hunk of bread. Mouse swallowed and tried not to feel the rumblings in her own empty belly. The puppeteer chewed slowly, whether in enjoyment of the unexpected repast or deep in thought, Mouse could not say. After a while the puppeteer brought out her knife and cut the tart neatly in two.

"The look on your face shames me, girl. Eat this and quit your pitiful staring."

Mouse quickly devoured the tart and licked her fingers clean. The puppeteer said, "That was a goodly feast, though one of your roasted hares is more to my liking." She smiled. "For all your faults, and they are legion, you have wormed your way into my affections. We are more alike than I imagined."

She tossed more wood onto the fire, sending a shower of bright sparks spiraling into the darkness. Then, leaning on the sturdy branch she used to poke the fire, she said, "Tell me, Mouse. How did you get that scar?"

Mouse related her story: how the almoner had caught her eating scraps at Dunston Manor and how Cook had raked his flesh hook across her face. How Simon and Alice and Claire had taken her to York, only to abandon her there. "So you see," she finished, "I cannot go back to Dunston."

"No, I suppose not. Still, there must be a better life for you than this."

"Mayhap that is so, but I cannot imagine it," Mouse said. "We go where we please, and when the summer fairs begin, our plays will make us rich as the king himself."

The puppeteer laughed. "If that is your plan, you will be sorely disappointed. Do you not know how reviled we are? Obscene, some folks say, and it is true some puppeteers use language unfit for gentle ears, though I myself take care never to offend." Taking her seat again, she said, "I have lost count of the number of times I have been run out of town, robbed, pelted with rotten fruit, all because I tried to tell a story and earn a few coins in the bargain. In Dover once I was offered a coin and a bed for the night in exchange for a promise not to perform. Mark my words, little one. You will never become rich as a puppeteer, though you be the best in all the realm."

"But you have capes and turbans, a goodly wagon, and the puppets."

"They once belonged to my father. God rest him."

"Then he was a puppeteer! What happened to him?"

Standing to poke the fire once again, the puppeteer said, "No more questions. We must be away early on the morrow."

Relieved that she would not be left behind again, Mouse watered the horse and banked the fire for the night, then went inside the wagon. From his perch on the trunk, the black-eyed sorcerer watched her every move.

"If it please you," she whispered, "cast a spell to make me smart instead of an addle brain."

Then she asked Sir Alfred, "What troubles my puppeteer so sorely that she weeps?"

She held the knight tightly, listening intently for his reply. But there was only the sound of the horse cropping grass and the distant notes of a shepherd's flute drifting on the wind.

CHAPTER EIGHT

The Goose Woman's Tale

The coin box was empty, and they had long since used the last of the flour and salt. As May warmed into June, all that remained of their meager stores was a tin of barley, half a jar of honey, and a few wormy apples. The puppeteer said there was money to be made at the fair in Reedham, but that was still a fortnight away.

They were camped in a wild glade thick with birch and oak trees. Nearby was a narrow stream that provided fresh water and the occasional trout for their supper. Mouse had grown adept at snaring game. Usually, it was a hare she roasted on the spit or made into soup flavored with wild roots, but once she trapped a pheasant, and the puppeteer had been so pleased, she danced around the fire. Mouse gathered the wild berries ripening along the stream, and they ate them by the handful.

Mouse practiced her carving on a small block of ash wood kept in her pocket and continued working with the puppets. After their chores were finished, the puppeteer would bring out the sorcerer or the princess or Sir Alfred.

"Make him kneel," she might say. And then she would watch, head tilted to one side in concentration, hands on her hips, while Mouse moved the strings ever so carefully till the knight was resting gracefully on one knee.

"Show me sadness," said the puppeteer one afternoon while they were practicing the story of King Arthur and Guinevere. Mouse pulled the wire. Bridget's head drooped.

"That will not do at all," the puppeteer said. "Our princess looks more sleepy than sad. Try again."

Mouse pulled another string to make the puppet's hands cover her eyes.

"Think, Mouse!" the puppeteer directed. "Think of the worst thing you can possibly imagine. Then show me how it would make you feel, were it actually to happen."

Mouse considered this. She had been sad to say good-bye to Alice, sad when Claire and Simon had left her in York, and sadder still when the puppeteer had left her on the road to Marlingford. But the worst thing?

That was not hard to imagine. If she lost her puppeteer, if something happened to her puppets, she could not live. The thought of it opened up a black hole inside her.

She moved Bridget's strings till the princess's shoulders sagged and the puppet collapsed inward with a grief that seemed to fill the very air around them.

"Just so," the puppeteer murmured. "Very good, Mouse. That is precisely how it feels."

She shook her head as if to dislodge an unwanted thought. "Enough. We must repair our dragon's tail. It is beginning to look most undragonly."

"Yes," Mouse said, setting Bridget carefully inside the trunk. "He said as much to me only yestermorn."

The puppeteer laughed. "It is a good thing no one can hear us in this wood, for they would surely think us mad, speaking of our puppets as though they live."

"They are alive to me," Mouse said simply.

"Yes. And it pleases me that you love them so. But you are growing up, Mouse. You should consider another kind of life. One with a family of flesh and blood instead of wood and wool."

"The puppets are enough family for you." Mouse closed the trunk. "If it please you, I must ask a question."

The puppeteer took out her needle and thread. "What do you wish to know?"

"Why must you hide the fact you are a woman? Is the eye patch naught but a part of your disguise? When I am a puppeteer, must I bind my hair and travel as a man?"

"That is three questions, by my reckoning." The puppeteer smiled ruefully. "I know of no law that forbids us the practice of our art."

"Then why—?"

"My reasons are best left unspoken. Bring the dragon here, will you, Mouse? Then fetch some water."

While the puppeteer worked on the dragon's tail, Mouse filled the bucket at the stream and returned to the wagon. Seating herself next to the puppeteer, she took out her carving and continued shaping a tiny likeness of Princess Bridget. Soon they heard voices. Two men were approaching from the westerly road. The puppeteer quickly drew her hood around her face and picked up her sword.

"Halloo!" one of the men called. He was a greasy, dirty man with small round eyes and a thin white scar trailing along one cheek. His companion wore a tattered cloak and a tangled gray beard that reminded Mouse of a rat's nest. Their shifty manner made Mouse uneasy. She slipped her hand into the puppeteer's.

The two men dropped their packs on the ground. The scar-faced one said, "I can tell from your wagon you are a pair who appreciate good entertainment. And we happen to be the best musicians in all of England. Normally, we perform only in the finest halls, but as it happens, we are on our way to a celebration in Wickham, and since we are here, we are prepared to make an exception. For the reasonable price of ten shillings, we will make you an evening of song and merriment you will never forget. What say you?"

"As you say, we are entertainers and well able to amuse ourselves," the puppeteer said.

"Five shillings. You may never have this chance again."

"If the fates are kind," the puppeteer muttered. "Go along. Leave us be."

"Upon my word!" the bearded man exclaimed, spying the little carving in Mouse's hand. "What is that?"

"It is only for practice," Mouse said.

"If it please you, may I see it?"

Mouse looked at the puppeteer, who shrugged and tightened her grip on the sword. Mouse handed him the miniature of Princess Bridget.

"A cunning little thing!" the man said, turning it over in his hand. "Quite charming. Just the thing for my young daughter. I will give you a ha'penny for it."

Mouse was tempted, for they needed any coin, no matter how small. But she shook her head.

"A penny, then."

"Surely your daughter is worth more than that," Mouse said boldly. "As you say, it is a charming thing. Normally, I charge ten shillings, but since you are a fellow entertainer, I am prepared to make an exception. Five shillings."

The puppeteer's eye went wide.

"Three shillings," the man countered.

"Four. You will never have another chance to buy so fine a piece. Think of your daughter's happiness. You cannot put a price on that."

"Done."

He handed Mouse the coins and said to the puppeteer, "Last chance to hear the sweetest tunes this side of heaven."

She shook her head again. The man tucked the carving inside his scuffed leather pouch. "Then we bid you good evening, sir."

When the two men were out of earshot, the puppeteer laughed till she was breathless. "Oh, Mouse, you are clever! 'Normally, I charge ten shillings.' Whatever made you think of that?"

"I gave him a dose of his own medicine!" Mouse declared. "And we need the money."

"Indeed we do. I had planned to rent the theater for our shows in Reedham. Folks there seem to like their entertainment indoors. And we can give ten shows a day no matter what the weather. But tell me, where did you learn to be so shrewd a bargainer?"

"At Dunston I listened to Cook bargaining with the peddlers," Mouse said with a grin. "Fenn said Cook never paid a goodly price for anything."

"You are a clever girl," the puppeteer said again, tucking the coins away. "Now, I am hungry. What will we have for our supper?"

While Mouse made soup and gathered berries, the puppeteer finished repairing the dragon's tail. After supper they sat by the fire, talking about the plays they would give once they arrived in Reedham.

"Mayhap we shall give them *Noah's Ark*," the puppeteer mused. "Come, I will show you how to make the floodwaters."

They climbed onto the stage. The puppeteer showed Mouse two wooden buckets resting on a hidden ledge, attached by means of ropes and pulleys. The larger one had holes in the bottom.

"Before the play begins, fill the smaller pail with water," the puppeteer said. "When the time comes for the flood, pull this rope. The smaller pail will tilt into the larger one, and the water draining through the holes will look like rain."

"It does not seem hard to do," Mouse said. "When

next we give Noah's play, I shall take charge of the flood."

"You must take care not to drown our customers," the puppeteer said, grinning. "Once, in Canterbury, many years ago, my rope broke, and the water poured right onto the head of the archbishop!" Handing Mouse the small pail, she said, "Fetch some water and we shall practice, for the water must fall just so, else it will soak our puppets and our audience."

The next morning the puppeteer woke Mouse earlier than usual. "Up you get. I have decided to go to Wickham."

Mouse rubbed the sleep from her eyes. "What about Reedham?"

"The Midsummer's Eve fair is still days away. If those two men spoke the truth about a celebration in Wickham, mayhap we can earn a coin or two in the meantime."

Mouse folded her blanket and smoothed her threadbare tunic. "Is it far?"

"I have been there only a few times, but if memory serves, we will be there before sunset."

"Suppose there is no celebration?" Mouse asked.

"That is the chance we take."

They each ate an apple, then set off for Wickham. When, at midafternoon, they stopped to rest, Mouse was hungry as a beggar and wished she might set a snare for some meat, but the puppeteer was eager to end their journey before nightfall. They filled their bellies with water and went on.

Presently they came to a crossroad. "Our journey is almost done," the puppeteer said, "for there lies the road to Depford."

Depford! Mouse peered down the narrow road. Mayhap the puppeteer would give her leave to visit Alice. Would the kindly goose woman remember her?

It seemed forever before they arrived at last in Wickham.

Halting the wagon near the Black Swan Inn, the puppeteer said, "Look after our things while I make some inquiries."

In a moment she returned. "We are in luck, Mouse. On the morrow the mayor celebrates his birthday, and all the town is invited. Surely some folk will be in need of a pleasant tale. We shall camp at the end of the road and make ready our play."

As soon as they unhitched the wagon, Mouse set her snares. But there was neither hare nor fowl for their evening meal. They boiled some barley and sweetened it with honey and went to bed hungry.

Morning came, bringing a cool rain and a visit from the constable. He rapped on the side of the wagon, and when the puppeteer opened it, he said gruffly,

"Gypsies are not allowed here. Move along."

"We are not gypsies!" Mouse said hotly. "We are the finest puppeteers in the realm."

"Puppeteers, magicians, jugglers, all the same to me," the constable said. "Your kind always causes trouble. We want none of that here."

"We are here for the mayor's birthday," the puppeteer replied. "If we go, you must send the others away too. I do not think the mayor will like it if all his entertainers are banished."

The constable's eyes traveled around the inside of the wagon. "Keep to yourselves, then, and be on your way before this day is done."

When he had gone, the puppeteer handed Mouse one of their precious coins. "Take this and buy some bread. Then come back straightaway."

On the street near the inn, Mouse found a baxter's stall and gave the woman her coin. She tucked the loaf under her arm and started back to the wagon.

A skinny boy in brown breeches and a matching cap ran into her path and gave Mouse a sudden shove that sent her reeling. "Out of my way, you gypsy knave."

"I am neither gypsy nor knave," Mouse said, tightening her hold on her bread. "Leave me be."

Another boy, short and stubby-limbed, joined the first. "'Leave me be!'" he mocked. "Are you frightened of us, you knotty-pated little ragpicker?"

The boys laughed. Mouse tried to push past them, but one hefted a sharp stone and hit her squarely above her eye. Blood trickled down her face.

She dropped her bread and swung at the shorter boy, landing a solid blow on his ear. He howled. Then the boy in brown tripped Mouse, and she fell facedown in the dirt.

Before she could rise, the boys began kicking her with their heavy boots.

"Mouse!" Suddenly the puppeteer was upon them, pushing the boys aside, helping Mouse to her feet.

"Gor!" cried the boy in brown. "Another rotten gypsy. The town is plagued with them as a dog with fleas!"

"And we must be rid of vermin!" the other boy said, scooping another handful of stones.

"Run, Mouse!" The puppeteer grabbed Mouse's hand. As they raced through a hail of stones toward the wagon, the hood of the puppeteer's cloak slid to her shoulders, revealing her thick silver braid.

No one noticed, save Mouse and a solitary figure watching from the upper window of the Black Swan Inn.

The puppeteer hurriedly cleaned Mouse's wound, then hitched the wagon. At the mayor's house a few musicians and jesters gathered despite the rain.

Sounds of laughter and music drifted on the air.

"You are disappointed, Mouse," the puppeteer said. "But did I not tell you this life is a hard one?"

Mouse burrowed inside her oiled cloak and pressed her palm to her throbbing head. "We should not run away. We should stay and give our play despite those hateful boys."

"'Tis not worth the trouble, though our pockets be nearly empty," the puppeteer declared. "This rain will keep the paying crowd away."

"Where shall we go now?"

"We cannot go far today. We will go back to the crossroad and wait there for the rain to stop. Mayhap in that wood we will have more luck with our snares."

Mouse waited till they were near the crossroad before she spoke. "If it please you, I would go to Depford to visit the goose woman Alice."

"In this weather?"

"I do not mind a little rain," Mouse said. "Mayhap the sun will come out before this day is done."

"Mayhap. But you must take care. It will not do to have you sick with fever when we get to Reedham."

By the time they reached the crossroad, the rain had indeed stopped. Ignoring the throbbing pain in her head, Mouse helped the puppeteer unhitch the horse, then hurried about, setting her snares. When that was done, she said, "If it please you, Teacher, I would be away."

The puppeteer laughed. "Go along, then. Follow that road. But watch how you go, Mouse. Do not talk to strangers and see that you are back before sundown. I should not like to think of you on the road alone after dark."

"I will be careful."

"Mouse? Your goose woman may be away, selling her geese at the market. You must not be too disappointed if you find she is not at home."

Mouse had not thought of that. But the chance to see Alice was one she might never have again. With a wave of her hand, she left the clearing and set off toward Depford.

The sun was high overhead by the time she entered the village. It was an ordinary town, like many of the others Mouse had seen in her travels. Close by the side of the road sat an inn and, farther on, a gray stone church with a pretty colored window, then a handful of thatched-roof cottages scattered like mushrooms across a rolling meadow. Along the main street a few merchants had opened their stalls; Mouse chose a friendly face and said to the man, "If it please you, sir, I am looking for the house of a goose woman called Alice. She is tall, and her hair is black, and—"

"Far end of the meadow," he said. "The cottage with the yellow door. But be careful of the geese. They are a bad-tempered lot."

Mouse raced toward the meadow. So much to tell Alice! So many questions bumping around in her head! She found the cottage and knocked.

"Who calls here?" came a voice from inside.

"It is Mouse, from the road to York. Do you remember me?"

Then the door opened, and there was Alice. "It cannot be! Is it truly my little Mouse? Dear me, what happened to your head? Do not tell me you fell off another oxcart."

"It is naught but a scratch," Mouse said, grinning.

"Come in, child! My, you have grown so tall these past months."

Alice led Mouse to a table piled high with pots and tins, which she quickly pushed aside. "First we will eat, and then you will tell me everything. Oh, I am so happy to see you! I have often wondered what became of you. Tell me, how is life in York?"

Before Mouse could answer, a fat goose wandered in, flapping and hissing.

"Henrietta!" Alice scolded. "Away with you! Can you not see we have company?"

Alice shooed the goose out the door and put a pot on

the fire. She bustled about, setting the table, rattling plates and cups and spoons. Soon Mouse was looking at more food than she had seen in a very long time. There was bread with butter and honey, a platter of roasted mutton, a bowl of stewed apples with raisins and spice. When Mouse had eaten two helpings of everything, Alice stoked the fire and buttered another piece of bread. "Now," she said, smiling at her young guest, "tell me everything."

"I do not live in York, but in a wagon upon the road. I am a puppeteer's apprentice."

Then she explained that Claire had gone with Lady Ashby, and Simon had left her in York, and described her plan to steal away atop the puppeteer's wagon.

"Such a daring scheme!" Alice exclaimed. "I would never be so brave as that!"

"You are as brave as you decide to be," Mouse said.

Alice laughed. "It seems I have heard that before. It pains me to think Simon left you without so much as a good-bye. But I suppose I should not be surprised. He is a pleasant enough traveling companion but no more trustworthy than a rat in a grain bin. Tell me, have you seen him since?"

"No," Mouse said. "But soon it will be Midsummer's Eve, and we will go to the fair in Reedham. My puppeteer says the town will be full of music makers then."

"This puppeteer," Alice said, frowning. "I hope he is a kindly sort and not one to take advantage of a trusting girl. I cannot say I like the notion of your traveling about in such a fashion."

"My puppeteer is a kindly companion and a goodly teacher. In Reedham I shall have a part in our show."

"I can see you are eager for that," Alice said. "But truly, Mouse, you are growing into womanhood. Surely you would wish to have a home and a family of your own."

"The wagon is my home, and the puppets are my family," Mouse said. She described Sir Alfred and Princess Bridget and the others in her little band. "I do not wish to seem a braggart, but my puppeteer and I are the finest in all of England."

"Many years ago there was a puppet master in these parts who was said to be the finest in all of England," Alice said. "But he came to a very sad end."

"What happened?"

"He and his companions were set upon by thieves and killed. In broad daylight! It was a very famous case. It was said one fellow survived, but, if that be true, no one has ever seen him. It remains a mystery after all these years."

Alice refilled Mouse's cup and went on. "Of course, who knows how much of the story is true? You know how people love gossip. Stories get bigger with each new telling till it becomes impossible to know where the truth lies."

Curious, Mouse asked, "What did the murderers look like?"

"Ah. Another mystery," Alice said. "They say one was a weaseley sort of a man with a scar on his face, but that description fits half the men in the realm. Perhaps none of it is true. Who can say?"

Mouse nodded. She had seen several such men in her travels, the last only two days ago.

"You look troubled, Mouse," Alice said. "I hope I have not upset you with my tale. It all happened so long ago, I am certain you and your puppeteer are quite safe." She spooned more stewed apples into Mouse's bowl. "Now, we shall speak of other things."

Mouse told Alice about the day she had broken Sir Alfred's wire and about the play she had ruined in Marlingford. "Because of me, our purse is empty," she said ruefully, "except for the coins from the carving I sold."

Alice laughed. "You must not be too hard on yourself. I should think it would be very difficult indeed to make a puppet dance."

"Oh, it is!" Mouse said. "I have practiced and practiced, and still I am ready for naught but the smallest of parts."

"Be patient," Alice advised. "These things take time."

Time! Mouse started and looked out the window. Already the sun lay low in the trees. "I must go!" she said. "I promised to be home before dark."

Alice rose and packed a bottle of honey, a hunk of cheese, and the rest of the bread. From a basket in the corner, she brought out fresh apples. Then she scooped some flour into a cloth bag and tied it with a bit of string. "Mayhap this will keep the wolf from the door till your play in Reedham."

Mouse felt a sting behind her eyes as Alice embraced her.

"Godspeed, little Mouse. Come again if you can."

Henrietta honked as if to say good-bye as Mouse started down the road. At the end of the lane, Mouse turned and waved to Alice, then started home.

By the time she arrived at the crossroad, the light was fading, the sun settling behind the gray-green trees. The puppeteer was not in the yard, nor at the stream. Mouse opened the door, and the puppeteer cried, "Surprise!"

Mouse dropped her bundle and stared. The puppeteer was holding a new tunic and a kirtle of soft blue wool.

"Your mouth hangs open like an unhinged basket," the puppeteer said, smiling. "I have been working on these at odd moments for some time. I decided this would be a good day to finish, while you were away."

"But—" Mouse was overcome. Never had she owned anything so fine.

"You cannot deny you need new clothes," the puppeteer said. "Mayhap you have been too busy with our puppets to notice, but you have quite outgrown that threadbare old tunic. See how your wrists hang below the sleeve? Come. Let us see if these fit."

Mouse donned her new clothes and twirled around. The kirtle whispered and settled softly about her ankles.

The puppeteer nodded, satisfied with her handiwork. "You look lovely, Mouse. Precisely as a young girl should when she celebrates her feast day."

Mouse was incredulous. "But I know not when I was born, nor how many a twelvemonth has passed since then."

"The cook once guessed you were eleven, did he not?"

Mouse nodded.

"Then I have decided: This is your feast day, and you are twelve. From now on, you will count your age from this day. I only regret we have no food for a proper celebration."

"But we do!" Mouse cried. "Alice has sent bread and cheese and, oh, I cannot remember what else, for I am too happy."

She hugged the puppeteer so tightly that for a

moment neither of them could breathe. Then the puppeteer pulled away and said gruffly, "Enough. Let us see
what food your friend has sent."

They spread their meal on a blanket before the fire
and ate and talked until dawn.

→ CHAPTER NINE ←

A Dream Fulfilled

The days passed so quickly that before Mouse knew it, Midsummer's Eve arrived and they were in Reedham. They left the wagon in the street outside the theater. Mouse carefully lifted the hem of her new kirtle and followed the puppeteer across the dirt yard, past a circular wooden gallery where the playgoers sat, then through a door at the front of the stage.

The theater roof was painted with a moon and stars. Wooden steps led to a wide platform with doors at either end. A ladder led to a second, smaller platform above the stage, equipped with winches and pulleys. Mouse and the puppeteer skirted a room filled with tables, chairs, hedges, false trees, and other props till they reached a windowed nook where the theater owner, a burly man with a thick gray beard, sat behind a desk.

"A puppeteer, you say!" he exclaimed when the puppeteer explained the purpose of their visit. "Are you any good?"

"Rent us your stage and judge for yourself," the puppeteer replied.

"What sort of plays do you propose?"

"Only the classics," the puppeteer said. "The story of Noah and of St. George and the dragon. Mayhap a tale from King Arthur's day. Nothing that will offend."

"I hope not!" the man said. "Last November we had a fellow who abused our ears with dirty jokes and stories not fit for decent folk."

"You will have no complaints about our plays," the puppeteer assured him. Opening her coin bag, she said, "How much for the rent?"

"A shilling a day and a penny for each ticket sold."

"A ha'penny per ticket," the puppeteer countered.

"Two days' rent will yield a tidy profit for us both."

"Done. Will you get our permit?"

"Wait here," he said. "I will return shortly."

Mouse listened to the music of flutes and tambourines coming through the open window. The smell of meat pies from the food sellers' stalls teased her nose, bringing with it memories of cold winter morns at Dunston when she had stirred the pots under Cook's watchful eye.

"Mayhap we will get a pork pie for supper, with

apples and raisins," Mouse said. "I am sorely tired of roasted hares."

"You may have whatever you wish," the puppeteer said, "for without your clever bargaining, we would have no coins for rent." She paused. "I am sorry I ever called you an addlebrained clod, for plainly you are not. And we must do something about your name. I am weary of calling you Mouse."

At that moment a dark face appeared at the window, so briefly that Mouse could not at first say whether it truly happened or was only imagined. But then the puppeteer gasped and spoke a single word. "Ordin!"

Beneath her hood the puppeteer's face went pale as wax, and it seemed to Mouse that there was suddenly an edge in the air, such as often foretells bad weather.

"Who was that man?" Mouse asked. "Do you know him?"

The puppeteer shook her head. "For a moment I thought it was someone I know, but surely I am mistaken."

The theater owner returned with a paper, and the puppeteer gave him the coins.

"Watch how you go," he said. "Midsummer's Eve, the town is full as a tick."

"Where may we leave our wagon?" the puppeteer asked.

He jerked a chubby thumb. "Beyond the mill is a meadow. It will be safe enough, but keep an eye out for thieves and troublemakers."

On the street again, Mouse and the puppeteer passed dancers and musicians, jugglers and jesters mixing with the crowd of villagers in town for the fair. Mouse would have liked nothing more than to watch the performers, but the puppeteer glanced furtively up and down the road, then grabbed Mouse's hand and said, sharply "Hurry along, girl. Stop your gawking and dawdling!"

Why was the puppeteer suddenly so jumpy?

"I am ready for the play," Mouse said. "Have I not practiced and practiced? I swear I will not disappoint you."

"I would not let you perform if I thought you were not ready," the puppeteer replied. "Now stop your prattling. There is work to be done."

When they were settled in the meadow, she handed Mouse the coin box and their banner. Then they carried their puppets' trunk the short distance down the alley to the back entrance of the theater. While the puppeteer was busy arranging Sir Alfred and the others behind the stage, Mouse tied their banner to the posts outside the door. Then she spread a blue cloth on the floor of the stage to represent a lake, arranging the folds till they resembled waves.

Presently a crowd gathered, and the puppeteer collected their coins. The playgoers streamed inside and took seats on the wooden benches. Soon the theater was full.

"A goodly crowd awaits your first play," the puppeteer whispered. "Ready, Mouse?"

Mouse fingered Bridget's strings and gave the puppeteer a shaky smile.

Dressed in a scarlet cloak and turban, the puppeteer spoke to the crowd. "Greetings. Our play this day is a story of Merlin and his mysterious arts, if you can conceive it, told by a mouse"—here she paused, turned, and winked at her apprentice—"if you can believe it."

Full of ale and good humor, the playgoers laughed. The curtain parted. Mouse took a quick breath to steady her hands and pulled the strings. Bridget strolled smoothly onto the stage. The crowd applauded.

The puppeteer moved Sir Alfred, dressed today as Merlin, onto the stage, then the puppet Noah, dressed as young King Arthur.

Holding Bridget still with one hand, Mouse slowly pulled with her other hand a string to which a tiny silver sword was attached, so that the sword appeared to be rising from the blue lake. "Ohh!" the audience breathed.

Mouse quickly fastened the sword's string to a hook hidden behind the curtain. Placing both her hands on Bridget's strings, she pulled gently, and Bridget, as the Lady of the Lake, spoke to Merlin. "You cannot get this sword."

"I know that," Merlin replied. The puppeteer nodded encouragingly to Mouse, then continued speaking in Merlin's voice. "As a favor to me, would you give the sword to my lord the king, for there is not in all the world a better use for it."

Mouse made Bridget bow, then said, "Surely your words be true. I will get the sword."

Working carefully, Mouse brought Bridget to the middle of the lake, where she grasped the sword, then turned to King Arthur. "Your sword, milord."

The puppeteer inserted the *pivetta* into her mouth and spoke as King Arthur. "My thanks, dear lady. May God grant us victory in the coming war."

Mouse scarcely felt the hot sun pouring through the high window or the ache in her arms as she held Bridget aloft. Almost before she knew it, the story ended, and the happy crowd spilled onto the street again.

With the sound of applause still ringing in her ears, Mouse was nearly drunk with joy. Seizing Sir Alfred, she danced around the stage, turning faster and faster till she was dizzy. Then she set him down, grabbed the puppeteer's hands, and swung her to and fro till they were both breathless and weak with laughter.

"Mayhap we should save our merrymaking till our work is done, little one," the puppeteer said. "We must give seven more plays before this day is done."

"I am so happy, I could give seven times seven!" Mouse declared. "Did you see how perfectly I made Bridget bow? Mayhap I am ready for a bigger part."

"Mayhap you are not!" the puppeteer retorted. "Now make haste. The next show begins soon."

The entire day passed as in a dream. The crowds ebbed and flowed in a ceaseless tide of color and laughter. By the time the last play ended and the puppets were safe inside their trunk, the sun had set and the air was full of good smells. A smoky haze from dozens of bonfires hung low over the meadow.

"We shall eat well this night," the puppeteer said, counting up their coins. "And you shall have an extra shilling to mark your first play."

"There is naught I need," Mouse said, full of pride and the satisfaction of hard labor well accomplished. "I made my puppet dance."

"Indeed," the puppeteer said, smiling. "But never refuse a coin, Mouse. For no one knows what the morrow may bring."

She handed Mouse a shilling. "This town is full of

revelers with too much ale in their bellies and too little sense in their heads. We must guard our belongings carefully, lest they be stolen in the night."

"I will guard us while you rest," Mouse said. "I am too full of happiness to sleep."

"I remember that feeling," the puppeteer said softly. "*Noah's Ark* was my first play. Father brought the story from Italy when he was but a boy."

"Which part was yours?"

"Oh, only one of the animals. The tiger, perhaps. A terrible disappointment, for I had begged to perform in the new play we were practicing. It was a story he spun himself out of our imagined past."

Such confidences from the puppeteer were pearls beyond price. Mouse dared not interrupt.

"We came from an ancient people called the Sabines," the puppeteer continued. "They were a very brave people who lived in the hills north of Rome. Father was working on the story of their battle with Horatius. He said it happened so long ago, I could not even imagine it. More than anything, I wanted to play the part of a Sabine warrior, with Sir Alfred as my puppet. But fate dealt us a cruel blow, and my chance was lost."

"What happened?"

"That is quite a sad tale, Mouse. And this is a night for making merry." She pressed more coins into

Mouse's hands. "Buy us something to eat. Anything you fancy will be all right with me. But do not dawdle, for I am hungrier than words can tell."

Mouse was hungry too, for more of the puppeteer's story, but she hurried toward the food sellers' stalls, past dancers in costumes of saffron, scarlet, and blue, past music makers with dulcimers and flutes and lyres. At the food sellers' she bought a pork pie, an apple tart, and a hunk of cheese.

She had taken but a few steps toward the wagon when she heard a rustling sound behind her. Turning quickly, she caught a glimpse of someone in the shadows. Was it one of the robbers the theater owner had warned against? Holding tightly to her sack, she darted into the noisy crowd.

"I am brave and strong," she whispered, turning this way and that. But at every turn the dark figure was still there. She thought of screaming, but who would hear her in such a boisterous crowd? She wheeled suddenly and ran in the opposite direction, nearly upsetting an old woman and her cart, shoving aside a dreamy-faced goat boy munching an apple.

A viselike hand grasped her shoulder. Caught!

Mouse flailed her arms and kicked for all she was worth till a familiar voice said, "Stop, Mouse, it is only me!"

Incredulous, she stilled and stared into the moss-green eyes of Simon Swann. "You!"

She balled a fist and landed a solid blow on his arm. "Why did you follow me? I took you for a thief or worse!"

"Mayhap someone followed you, but it was not I. I was entertaining these folk with the song I made for you. Do you remember?"

"I remember." Mouse was too happy at the unexpected reunion to be truly angry with Simon, but she said, "And I remember how you left me alone in York and ran away like a thief in the night!"

"Guilty as charged!" he said cheerfully. "But surely you know naught save the direst of circumstances could have torn me from your side. Tell me how you came to Reedham and where you will go on the morrow."

"I am the puppeteer's apprentice," she said, sweeping into a low bow. "Stories of bravery and romance, our specialty. As you wish."

"So! It was you who gave that show in the theater today."

"It was naught but a small part. And you were there! Why did you not show yourself before now?"

"I arrived late and left early, for I was busy earning a few coins for my own pocket. 'Twas a happy surprise to spot you in this crowd just now. Tell me your new name."

"I am still called Mouse."

"Oh, well. A name must not be chosen lightly. The right one will come in good time. Meanwhile, I am hungry as a beggar and in need of some good company to pass this night."

Then Mouse felt a tug on her sleeve.

"There you are!" the puppeteer said sharply. "Did I not tell you to hurry, Mouse? And who is this stranger?"

Before Mouse could explain, Simon bowed. "Good evening, sir. Simon Swann. Minstrel, juggler, and jester, just as you wish."

"I wish to be left alone," the puppeteer snapped. "Come along, Mouse. This one should not be trusted."

"Harsh words, but mayhap I deserve them," Simon said. "Still, it was I who rescued this maid from certain death upon the road. I cannot say I quite approve of her traveling with the likes of you."

"You know far less of me than you imagine," the puppeteer said, taking Mouse's arm. "Leave us, if you would start the morrow with both your ears."

Simon laughed. "And who would relieve me of them, pray tell?"

In less time than it takes to tell it, the puppeteer drew her sword and held the tip of it just beneath his ear. His eyes widened. "By my faith! I have seen that sword before!"

"You are mistaken, sir." As quickly as the puppeteer had drawn her sword, she concealed it beneath her cloak. "Will you come now, Mouse?"

Mouse wanted to tell Simon about all her adventures, but she could not disobey the puppeteer, who had turned on her heel and was marching purposefully toward the meadow. Simon fell into step beside them.

"It happened on the road in Staffordshire, just after Midsummer's Eve, why it must be ten summers ago at least. I came upon a troupe of vagabond performers returning from the London fair. I would have passed the night in their company, as travelers often do, but they seemed in haste and went on despite the dark, while I slept in a barn beside the road."

They reached the wagon. The puppeteer set out the food Mouse had bought and added a log to their fire. "We do not care one farthing for this tale and would eat our meal in peace."

"An entertaining story makes a goodly repast even more so," Simon said. "Though I will admit this one has no happy ending."

"Then spare us the telling, for the world is much too full of sorrow."

Mouse touched the puppeteer's hand. "If it please you, let him stay. Without him, I would have perished on the road from Dunston."

The puppeteer held up her hands in a gesture of surrender.

Simon said, "My thanks, Mouse!" He reached for their loaf of bread. "You will not mind my having a small bite, will you, as long as I am here?"

He chewed for a moment. "Anyway. The next morn I resumed my journey and had gone but a little distance when I heard in the road ahead a commotion such as I had never before heard. It was as if the gates of hell had opened there on the dusty road. I hid in the trees, where I could observe in secret. What do you suppose I saw, little Mouse?"

"I cannot guess." She took a bite of pork pie.

"It was those hapless vagabonds, set upon by a pair of highwaymen. In broad daylight!"

Suddenly Mouse's food stuck in her throat. Was not this the same story Alice had told, about the death of the puppet master? Could her puppeteer have been among that unfortunate troupe? Mouse stole at glance at the puppeteer, who sat quite still and spoke not a word.

Simon went on. "I would have been killed myself had I not taken refuge in the wood. When it was over, I went to the poor travelers in hopes of giving aid, but they were all dead and stripped of all their valuables, save a sword that had no doubt fallen unnoticed into the underbrush during the fray. I remember it well. A silver-handled sword it was, carved with a three-headed beast. Part wolf, part lion, part dog. I have never seen another like it. At first I thought to keep it, but in the end, my nobler nature prevailed. I buried the dead there in the wood and left the sword to mark their graves." He paused. "Mouse, would you spare a bite of cheese? And mayhap a smidgen of that apple tart?"

Dazed by the story and what it might mean, Mouse absently filled his plate. When Simon had taken a few more bites, he said, "A rumor went around that one of the unfortunates had escaped with his life and taken the sword with him. And it is true that on my return the following month it was gone. Still, the chance of anyone surviving the events of that morn seem as likely as a St. Swithin's Day blizzard."

"I quite agree," the puppeteer said quickly. "A preposterous tale. Again, Swann, I beg your leave. We are weary and have much to do on the morrow."

"As you wish." Simon rose. "Though I was looking forward to hearing about your adventures, Mouse. Mayhap we shall meet again, when your companion is more agreeable."

Mouse caught his sleeve. "I have been to visit Alice in Depford. But I have no news of Claire."

"Ah. Dear Alice. As full of gossip as ever, I wager. I

have no news of Claire, but I am certain she fares well. If I chance upon her, I will give her your greeting straightaway." To the puppeteer he said, "I would sing you a song in payment for my supper, if it please you."

"It would please me if you would leave us in peace," the puppeteer returned.

But Simon took out his lute anyway. "It will take but a moment to erase the debt I owe." He began to sing:

"On the road to London town, I met a maiden fair.
She wore a snow-white linen gown, and ribbons in her
*   hair.*
Her brown eyes shone like summer rain, oh, ne'er shall I
*   forget.*
Because she did not have a name, I called her Vi-o-let."

Though the puppeteer clapped politely, Mouse could tell from her mentor's pinched smile that she was eager to be rid of their unbidden guest.

"Good-bye, Mouse," Simon said. "When next we meet, mayhap you will have a proper name."

"Mayhap we will never meet again," Mouse said. "You come and go like a sparrow on a fence, just as you will."

"True enough," Simon admitted. "But how about this: Let us make a pact to meet here, on this very spot, a twelvemonth from today. You and your puppeteer shall make a new play for my entertainment, and for my part, I shall sing three new songs. Mayhap four, if you ask politely enough."

"We shall see what fortune decrees," the puppeteer said. "For now, we would bid you farewell."

When Simon was gone, Mouse gathered their plates, her head fairly swimming with questions about his remarkable story. But the puppeteer seemed jumpy and in no mood for talk.

"That was a goodly feast," she said to Mouse, "and now I would sleep. Keep your eyes open and wake me at once should anyone approach."

Mouse rekindled the fire. "I wonder if Simon's story be true."

"Did you not tell me his preposterous story of being bitten by a crocodile in India? And did you notice this night how he made himself the hero of his own tale? One day he will speak falsely to the wrong person, and we shall find his handsome head set upon London Bridge." Cupping Mouse's chin in her hand, she said, "It seems to me he is full of unbelievable tales. Think no more of it. On the morrow we shall give our play again, and Simon Swann will be well forgotten."

One by one, the bonfires in the meadow flickered out, till the only light came from the pale moon and twinkling stars. Lying on her blanket beneath the inky sky,

Mouse went over the events of the day in her mind. The happy crowds clapping for her—the puppeteer's apprentice. Then her fright when she thought she was being followed. And Simon's strange tale that, despite the puppeteer's protests, somehow had the ring of truth.

She rose and peered into the wagon. All was stillness and shadows. She opened the door. The puppeteer's face was serene in sleep, bathed in the splash of moonlight coming through the window.

Mouse dropped noiselessly to her hands and knees and crept along the floor till her fingers closed over the cold blade of the sword. It was much heavier than she had imagined, requiring all her strength to lift it. She carried it outside.

"Oh!" she cried.

For there, barely visible in the moonlight, was the three-headed beast. Part wolf. Part lion. Part dog. Just as Simon had described it.

→ CHAPTER TEN ←

Marbury Wood

One gray morning at the end of October, the puppeteer woke Mouse just before sunup. "Make haste," she said. "While you slept, a stranger passed with news of a celebration at Gimingham. If the good duke still holds those lands, mayhap he will bid us pass All Hallows' Eve there in exchange for a play."

Mouse struggled from sleep and sat up, drawing her blanket close against the morning chill. "Would the duke have aught to do with vagabonds like us?"

The puppeteer darted about the wagon, folding her blanket, taking out the pots for their morning meal. From their store of provisions gathered during their treks to the summer fairs, she took out a flask of honey and measured a handful of barley into the cooking pot. Beneath her shapeless garment Mouse saw the outline of the sword. Curiosity burned like a Midsummer's bonfire inside Mouse, but in all the time that had passed since Simon had told his strange tale, she dared not reveal what she knew of the silver saber and its mysterious markings. All summer long her mentor had seemed jumpy and preoccupied. Often they had left town hurriedly, the wagon bumping along darkening roads with naught but the surefooted horse and the sputtering lantern to guide them.

Now the puppeteer said, "The duke was a friend of my father, though many a twelvemonth has passed since then." She handed Mouse the water bucket. "Fill this, then make a goodly fire, for a cold wind blows this morn."

Mouse dressed quickly and complied, and soon a fire crackled in the clearing in Marbury Wood, where they had passed a quiet night. When the boiling barley thickened, they ladled it into their bowls and sweetened it with honey.

"How far to Gimingham?" Mouse queried. A silvery fog was seeping through the trees, bringing with it an unease that made her shiver. "I should not like to be in this wood on All Hallows' Eve. Fenn said that is the time evil walks about."

"Two days' journey along the easterly road will bring us to the manor," the puppeteer replied. "If the stranger's words prove true, we shall find ourselves in the midst of a celebration and away from harm till the day is safely past."

"Will there be wassail for All Hallows' Day?" Mouse wondered. "At Dunston I helped Cook make it, but never would he give me leave to taste it."

"The duke will provide a goodly feast, and wassail there will be, full of roasted apples and spice."

"With sweet cakes floating on top?" Mouse could nearly taste the savory treat.

"With sweet cakes floating on top."

"We shall give our play, and mayhap the duke will bid us stay till Christmas," Mouse said. "I should like to play some games and listen to the harps. Mayhap there will be roasted goose for supper and jesters and music makers all the way from London."

The puppeteer smiled. "First we must go to Gimingham and see whether a welcome awaits. Finish your meal. The sun is nearly up, and we must be away."

While they ate, they spoke of the new play they would give in the spring and of the puppets themselves, which seemed more than ever like living beings, so dearly did Mouse love them.

"Sir Alfred needs a new costume," Mouse said, licking clean her spoon. "His old one is so full of holes, he is quite embarrassed. I shall make him a new one. Mayhap then Bridget will think him the finest knight in all the realm."

"Perchance she will. Then again, one never knows what our princess will do. But mayhap her unpredictability is part of her charm."

"I think she only pretends not to love Alfred." Mouse broke off a bit of bread and mopped the last drop of honey from the bottom of her bowl. "Have you noticed our dragon needs a new head?"

"Quite so. He has grown so cracked and faded, he does not look fierce at all. I should not be surprised to find him weeping into his pillow for the shame of it, poor fellow."

Then the two of them laughed merrily, their voices clear and pure as the notes of a lyre.

"I shall never forget the day you flung poor Alfred onto the dragon's back," the puppeteer said ruefully. "It is a wonder we were not flogged, so angry was that crowd." Her one blue eye held steady on her young companion. "You have learned much since then, little one, and acquitted yourself far beyond the promise of your years."

It was true, Mouse thought with a deep sense of pride. In the long months since stealing aboard the wagon, she had, through mistakes and hard work, proven worthy of her art and earned the right to call herself the puppeteer's apprentice.

The puppeteer went on. "I have never seen a finer

performance than the one you gave at the Derby fair on St. Swithin's Day. Bridget fairly glided across the stage to meet St. George. It is an apt pupil you are, and I do regret having misjudged you."

"I misjudged you," Mouse said. "Before I knew you were not a man, I thought surely you were a dangerous outlaw, or else a rogue prince, traveling in disguise."

"Ha!" The puppeteer shook her head. She warmed her hands before the fire. "Mayhap we shall choose a name for you today, for it is plain to me you never were a mouse."

Full of emotion, Mouse said fervently, "I would share your name, if you would reveal it."

In a voice suddenly frigid as the morn, the puppeteer said, "I have given you the knowledge you were bound to learn, but never will I give you my name."

Stung, Mouse said, "Keep it, then! I would not have it now for all the gold in the world."

"It is always easy to despise what you cannot have." The puppeteer began gathering their bowls. "Douse the fire, Mouse, then hitch the—"

Her words were swallowed up in the thunderous sound of hoofbeats that suddenly filled the clearing. Two riders dressed in black raced through the wood, their swords and poleaxes gleaming dully in the watery autumn light. One was fat and red-faced. The other, racing pell-mell behind, seemed in his saddle to be tall as a giant. Before Mouse could move or make a sound, the men were upon them.

"Run, Mouse!" the puppeteer cried, taking up her sword.

But Mouse could only stand there, her mouth suddenly bone-dry, all her senses sharpened by fear. She was aware all at once of the smell of smoke and lathered horses and the fearsome gleam of the weapons against the muted colors of their wagon. The snap of the logs burning in the campfire seemed to roar in her ears.

With a bloodcurdling yell, the fat man drew his sword. The clearing rang with the screech of blade on blade as the puppeteer fought for her life. Mouse finally found her feet. She ran to the wagon and crouched beneath it just as the giant turned his horse and, with a vicious blow from his poleax, splintered the roof. Shards of green paint and bare wood rained down and collected in the folds of Mouse's kirtle. She watched in horror as the man seized their horse and, with a single motion, drew his sword from throat to belly. The terror-stricken animal screamed and crumpled onto the frosted earth, his sides heaving, his dying breath clouding the air.

Another scream echoed in the clearing. Mouse

peered from beneath the wagon. Somehow, the puppeteer had unseated the fat man from his mount. Now she attacked from behind with a mighty blow that felled him at last and sent his horse running down the road.

The giant wheeled his horse and charged toward the puppeteer, his thick curls flying like a black pennant in the wind. Mouse saw a quick flash of metal as his poleax went spinning through the air.

Mouse tried to yell a warning, but no sound came. Dizzy with fear, heaving with silent sobs, she could but watch as the weapon buried itself in the puppeteer's shoulder, and the puppeteer fell. Then the giant dismounted and began ransacking the wagon, tossing aside the puppets and their wooden chest, rolls of cloth and the paint pots, then their blankets, bowls, and flasks.

The puppeteer tried to rise, but the effort was too much. She moaned, a pitiful, desperate sound. Mouse gulped air and tried to clear her mind. She must do something before it was too late. Her heart pounded wildly. On her hands and knees beneath the wagon, she edged closer to the murderous thief.

He was crouched in the dirt, muttering to himself as he raided their money box. The fog-shrouded clearing now was so quiet, Mouse could hear the faint tinkling of the coins spilling onto the ground.

Soundlessly, she edged closer still, till she could

see his scuffed black boots and the frayed hem of his cloak. Gathering her courage, she rolled from beneath the wagon.

His horse shied and nickered softly, but the man continued his pilfering. Mouse leapt to her feet, seized a burning branch from the fire, and raised it above her head. At that moment the man turned, and Mouse stared, thunderstruck, into the eyes of the man she had first encountered at the ribbon seller's stall in Marlingford. There was no mistaking the silver medallion hung about his neck. As surely as if she had been dealt a blow, Mouse realized it was his face she had glimpsed at the window of the theater in Reedham, his face that had so terrified her puppeteer. Now she knew his name.

"Ordin!" she cried.

"Put down that branch, girl. I have no quarrel with you." He spoke quietly, as if to calm her. "It is your companion I have sought, for she is the one whose word sent me to prison for more years than I care to remember."

"It *was* you who followed us all summer and frightened my puppeteer!"

He smiled. "Biding my time till I could catch you alone, without the protection of crowds at the fairs. Your puppeteer is a slippery sort. More than once I lost your trail, but I do not give up easily."

"Mouse!" the puppeteer cried faintly. But Mouse dared not take her eyes off Ordin. She tightened her grasp on the burning branch. Suddenly Ordin reached for his dagger, which lay but an arm's length away, but desperation fueled Mouse's quickness. She jabbed the red-hot ember squarely into his eye, then landed a solid blow on his head.

With a roar, he flailed his arms and stumbled about the clearing, then toppled into the crackling fire. Flames licked at his cloak and his breeches. He rolled away and began crawling blindly toward the stream, but soon he collapsed and lay still. The stench of charred flesh hung heavily in the air.

Mouse stood there, tears streaming down her face. She dropped the burning branch and rushed to the puppeteer, who lay facedown, one arm outstretched, the other protecting the sword lying beneath her. The blade of Ordin's poleax was deeply embedded in her shoulder. Despite the fire, Mouse had never in all her life felt so cold. The smells of blood and death made her stomach roil. "Think!" she ordered herself, and then it seemed the very air around her shimmered with the knowledge of what she must do.

"I will go to Gimingham." The sound of her own voice steadied Mouse as she moved about the clearing. She gently lifted the puppeteer's arm and freed her sword.

The blade was nicked and slick with blood, but Mouse was beyond shock. With the hem of her kirtle, she calmly wiped it clean, then bent over the bodies of the dead thieves to see what useful things might be found. She took Ordin's dagger, then bent over his companion, who also lay facedown, one leg crumpled beneath him. Reaching under his hulking form, Mouse extracted a leather pouch bulging with coins and a flask that smelled of strong spirits.

Carefully, she turned the puppeteer onto her side and lifted the puppeteer's head. "Drink this."

She dribbled the amber-colored liquid into the puppeteer's mouth. "You must lie still. I will go to Gimingham and find someone to aid us."

The puppeteer nodded. "Watch how you go. Ordin—"

"Dead," Mouse reported. "And his companion, too. But I will leave Ordin's dagger here, should you have need of it."

She covered the puppeteer with their blankets, then gathered the puppets, stuffing them hastily into two empty flour sacks from the wagon. She retrieved Ordin's wild-eyed horse from the thorny underbrush and coaxed him back into the clearing. Then, with the leather straps used for securing their trunks, she tied the puppeteer's sword and her puppets onto the saddle and climbed up.

Beneath his unaccustomed rider the horse pranced nervously. Mouse did not think about her fright the time she had fallen from the peddler's horse. Her only thought was to save her puppeteer. Leaning forward, she patted the curve of the horse's neck. "There now," she crooned, as much to steady her own racing heart as his. "I will not hurt you. Get along, horse, and be quick about it."

Digging her heels into his sides, she urged him onto the road.

CHAPTER ELEVEN

Gimingham

At the far end of Marbury Wood, there is a crossroad leading east and west, and it was upon this road some time later that Mouse overtook a farmer with his oxcart.

"I pray you, sir," she said, reining in the lathered horse, "how far to the manor house at Gimingham?"

"A hard ride will find you there by sundown," he replied. "But beware how you go. There are strangers about. And look after that horse. He will not last the journey without water and rest."

Mouse thanked the man and started off again, the awkward bundles bumping against the saddle. The fog had burned away, and a weak autumn sun shone as she rode on and on down the empty road. It seemed days had passed since the events of the morning; her arms and legs felt heavy, as if she had not slept for a twelve-month.

"Sir Alfred," she asked aloud, "what will become of us?"

But he made no answer.

Near midday Mouse stopped to rest and water the horse at a stream running beside the road, and again as the afternoon light waned. It was nearly dark when the lights of a manor house appeared through the trees.

She dismounted and led the horse by the reins up the curving lane, past farmers still working in the fields, past the malt house, the smithy and stable, till she reached a tall iron gate. Before she could call out a greeting, the gatekeeper approached, his torch raised.

"Who goes there?"

"Please, sir. If this be Gimingham, I must see the duke. It is a matter of life and death."

"What is this?" he asked, looking past her into the approaching darkness. "Some scheme to draw me out until your accomplices can slip inside?"

"It is no scheme. I am alone. I myself was set upon by thieves just this morn, and my companion lies wounded in Marbury Wood. I pray you, send help before it is too late."

"A clever ruse, sending a child to beguile me with a pitiful tale." The man held his torch closer to Mouse. "But that scar belies your story, girl. Go away."

A round man in a neat brown beard hurried toward the gate. "What is it, Paston?"

"This child claims to be a victim of thieves in Marbury Wood and begs our aid for her companion, who has fallen there. A scheme, no doubt, dreamed up by those highwaymen who have been spreading their terror these past days. They mean to rob us, I trow."

Mouse stepped into the circle of guttering torchlight. "If it please you, sir, I must find the duke at once."

"You have found him," the man said with a slight bow. "I am Thomas of Gimingham. So, set upon by thieves, you say?"

Mouse nodded. "Two of them. My companion, whose father was your friend long ago, is gravely wounded and begs your aid."

The gatekeeper laughed. "A preposterous tale, meant for an All Hallows' trick or worse. Send this urchin on her way, or else hold her here till the sheriff can be summoned."

"Wait a moment." The duke opened the gate.

"What are you doing?" the gatekeeper cried. "Her accomplices may lie in wait in the dark."

Ignoring his gatekeeper, the duke said to Mouse, "Where did you get this horse?"

"It belonged to the thief," Mouse said impatiently. "He killed our horse and sundered our wagon, and he would have destroyed our puppets, too, if only—"

"Puppets?" the duke interrupted.

"Yes, sir. If you please, go to Marbury Wood, in the clearing near the easterly road, and you will see I speak the truth."

"I recognize the trappings on this horse," the duke told his gatekeeper. "They are those of Ordin, who is wanted for a dozen crimes hereabouts. Go at once and mount a party to fetch this child's companion, then alert the sheriff. Mayhap there is still time to catch the thieves before they do more harm."

"You will not need the sheriff," Mouse said. "Both the thieves are dead."

With a smirk, the gatekeeper said, "Felled by your own brave hand, no doubt."

"Only one of them," Mouse said matter-of-factly. "My companion killed the other."

The gatekeeper burst into peals of laughter. "I must say, this tale grows more unbelievable by the moment. Surely, sir, you can see this is but a trick to lure us away and render our house unprotected."

"It will not take an army, Paston, to retrieve one wounded soul. Enough men there be to guard us in your absence. Make haste and send for me as soon as you return."

So saying, he swung wide the gate. And Mouse, tired, hungry, and afraid for the fate of her dear puppeteer, went inside.

• • •

Pale sunlight was streaming through a high window when Mouse awoke. Startled, she sat up in the strange bed. Her clothes were gone, replaced by a soft nightdress she did not recall having donned. From below came the drone of voices and the sound of horses on the road. Then she remembered everything.

Before she could rise, there was a knock at the door, and in came a thin young woman carrying a basin and pitcher. Folded neatly over one arm were Mouse's tunic and kirtle. "You are awake at last," she said.

"Have the men returned from the wood?"

"At dawn this morn, and bearing your companion, just as you said."

"Does she— is she—?"

"Alive for the moment, though my lord says her wound is quite grave. All in this house are at prayer for her. We have tended her wounds and summoned the physician from the abbey. And the men have brought your wagon back. There is nothing more to be done."

Mouse threw back the coverlet. "I must see her."

"Wait awhile, till she wakes. I have brushed your clothes and brought water for washing up." She smiled. "You were so tired last night, I merely stripped off your clothes and tucked you in without a wash, though Nurse Catchpole did not approve."

"I thank you for your kindness."

The girl bobbed her head, then set the basin down. "When you are dressed, I shall have Cook make a goodly meal to warm your insides."

"I cannot eat. Worry has stolen my appetite, as surely as a thief."

"We must pray for God's mercy," the girl said, placing Mouse's clothes on the bed. "In the meantime, your sword and your puppets are safe in that trunk in the corner. Your horse is in the stable, but my lord says you will want different trappings before you ride again." She turned toward the door. "He says you are to ask for anything you need."

"There is aught I need but my puppeteer," Mouse said.

When the maid had gone, Mouse tumbled from the bed and opened the trunk. There lay her beloved puppets in a dirty tangle of shattered limbs, broken strings, and tattered costumes that smelled strongly of smoke. She gathered them all into her arms. "I will not cry," she whispered, "but I am sore afraid."

The sorcerer's head tilted to one side, as if he were listening. Mouse gazed intently into his black eyes. "If it please you," she said thickly, "cast a spell to make our puppeteer well, for I cannot live without her."

Then the door opened and a small voice said, "Oh!"

In came a little girl of no more than seven summers. She set the tray she carried on the chair and tiptoed across the room. "Oh, they are wondrous. If it please you, may I touch them?"

Mouse wiped her eyes. "You must take care, for they are very old, and now they are broken, as you can see." She lifted Sir Alfred, who had lost an arm in the fray. "This one is my favorite."

"Are they magic?" the girl asked.

"I once thought so. But I have learned the real magic lies in the happiness they bring to others."

"Will you give a show for us?"

"When my puppeteer is well again."

"Nurse Catchpole says the wound is mortal, but we must pray all the same."

For the first time since her ordeal began, Mouse allowed herself to consider all she would lose if her puppeteer should leave her. "She *will* live. And if you wish to see my puppets again, you will speak no more of death."

"Forgive me," the child said prettily. "Surely you are right." She touched Sir Alfred's damp, smoky cloak. "What happened to his other arm? Why does that wire come from his head? Will you show me how he works?"

"Mayhap another day."

"On the morrow?"

"I cannot promise."

"For All Hallows', then," the girl said, her eyes alight with mischief. "I should like a play with witches and ghosts, if it please you. Something scary to shiver the bones and send Nurse Catchpole screaming from the room in terror."

"Lunette?" a woman called from the hallway.

"Nurse Catchpole! I must go!" The girl waggled her fingers at Mouse and hurried away.

CHAPTER TWELVE

The Puppeteer's Tale

"She has awakened," the duke told Mouse on a cold morning three days later. "She is very weak but begs your presence straightaway."

Setting aside the new head she was carving for the dragon, Mouse rose and drew the puppeteer's gray cloak tightly about her shoulders. Despite the fire crackling in the grate, the stone walls of her bedchamber seemed to hoard the chill wind that had the night before dusted all of Gimingham with snow.

"I must apologize for failing to look after you properly," he said as they left the room and continued along the corridor. "My thoughts have been so taken by the plight of your companion, I have quite forgotten everything else. Is there aught you need?"

"I am well, sir."

He nodded. "My daughter, Lunette, has spoken of nothing but your puppets since the day you arrived. If

her attentions become too burdensome, you have but to
say so."

"She is no burden," Mouse said, hurrying to keep up
with his long strides. "Tell me, how fares my puppeteer?"

He stopped before the door to a bedchamber and
fixed her with a kindly gaze. "You seem a sensible
young woman, so I shall speak plainly. Her wound is so
grave, I cannot believe she will live. Still, such matters
are not for mortals to decide."

He opened the door. Mouse rushed to the bed where
the puppeteer lay, looking pale and insubstantial as
moonlight, her silver hair like a halo around her head.
Against the white linen her black eye patch was stark as
a lump of coal in snow.

"Mouse." Slowly, the puppeteer's blue eye opened,
and she smiled wanly. "You are not harmed. But what
of our puppets?"

Holding tightly to the puppeteer's hand, Mouse said,
"Sir Alfred has lost an arm, and most of the others are
dirty and broken. But they are safe." She swallowed the
hard lump in her throat. "And your sword is safe too,
but the wagon will want repair when you are well."

Tears spilled down the puppeteer's cheek. She closed
her eye.

The duke motioned Mouse to a chair beside the fire.

"Sit here, my dear. Your puppeteer bids me tell you this tale, which begins many years ago, when I was young and newly installed in these parts."

Mouse sat but kept her gaze fastened on the puppeteer.

"One evening," the duke began, "I came upon a band of travelers who had stopped for the night in an abandoned church near Marbury Wood. It was very late and very cold. The travelers welcomed me to their fire and shared their meat and drink, though they had little to spare.

"In this troupe were a minstrel or two, a jester, and a puppet master and his young daughter. She was a winsome sprite in a crimson cloak, with silver-colored braids and eyes so blue, they put the flowers to shame. After we had supped, she climbed onto her father's wagon and, with her puppets, performed the story of Jason, who made rain by casting water upon a sacred stone."

Mouse nodded. She had learned the story of Jason and the wondrous tasks he performed in his quest for the golden fleece just after Midsummer's Eve, when a week of rain held her and the puppeteer captive inside the wagon.

"Later that night I became so ill, I thought I might die. When morning came, the others in the troupe resumed their journey, but the puppet master and his daughter stayed behind to care for me."

The bedchamber door opened, and Lunette came in balancing a tray laden with cups of ale, a bowl of steaming broth, and a plate of raisin cakes. "Cook says you must eat."

"And so we shall," the duke said. "But you should be at your music lessons, Lunette."

"Chords and scales! Pray tell, Father, how can I possibly concentrate on anything so boring while there is a real puppeteer in the house?" She grinned. "I gave the serving girl a ha'penny to let me come in her stead." To Mouse she said, "Have I not been patient for three entire days? When will you show me how to make the puppets dance?"

"This is hardly the time to beg favors," the duke told her. "Go along now and leave this young woman in peace."

When Lunette had gone, he handed Mouse a cup, then took up the bellows and tended the fire till the flames rekindled. "Where was I?"

"The puppeteers stayed behind to look after you," Mouse prompted.

"Quite so. The next evening Ordin, enraged that I had recently recovered some land he had stolen from me, overtook me and set upon me with fist and dagger, despite my weakened condition."

"Coward," Mouse muttered.

"Indeed. And to think he was once a respected landowner, a friend to our king, till he fell out of favor and was overcome by bitterness. Never before had a man looked at me with such hatred. Had it not been for the puppet master and his daughter, I would not have lived to tell this tale."

The bedcovers rustled, and the puppeteer opened her eye again. "Father was very brave."

"As were you, my dear," the duke said. To Mouse he said, "Though they had no weapons save a spade and the rocks lying in the field, they fought my attacker and spared my life. This only enraged Ordin further. He shouted at me that he would not rest till I lay dead and all these lands were his. But in his enforced absence my holdings grew till it would have been impossible to usurp my land, with all my men here to guard it. I can only suppose he began then to live for revenge against those who had saved my life."

"That morning in the wood," Mouse began, frowning, "Ordin said it was my puppeteer who had sent him to prison."

The duke nodded. "She and her father witnessed against him for the attack on me in the churchyard, and he was sent away. Thankful for their aid, I sought them out at the fair in Reedham and gave them a silver sword as a token of my gratitude."

"Besides our puppets, it was the thing Father held most dear in this world," the puppeteer murmured.

"That is not quite so," the duke said gently. "You were his greatest treasure." He lifted his own sword from a table near the fire and placed it in Mouse's hands. "The carving is meant to represent the three faces of time. The wolf devours the past, the lion gives courage for the present, and the dog is a faithful companion for the future."

"Come closer, Mouse," the puppeteer rasped.

Mouse knelt at the puppeteer's bedside.

"I would not leave you with a wrong impression of your friend Simon Swann," the puppeteer said. "Though I tried to discredit his story, it is mostly true. Some years after the duke had given us the sword, Father and I were on our way to a fair in Staffordshire when we were set upon by three men, just as Swann told. Two were strangers, but the third was Ordin. He beat Father unmercifully, and when I went to Father's aid, Ordin attacked me with his dagger. Though I was badly hurt and blinded in one eye, I hid in the wood and escaped with my life. Father and the two musicians traveling with us were not spared."

The duke brought the puppeteer the bowl of broth and held her shoulders while she tried to sip it.

"Hush now and sleep," he said. "The rest of this tale will wait upon another day."

But the puppeteer continued. "Someone, mayhap it was Swann, buried them deep in the wood and left Father's sword to mark the graves. When darkness fell, I retrieved the sword. As soon as I was able, I disguised our wagon with paint from our pots. I bound up my hair and, from that day to this, traveled as a man." She stopped to recover her breath, then went on. "I have spent my life looking over my shoulder, knowing Ordin would not rest till he had found me, too."

"But surely some kind family would have taken you in," Mouse said. "The duke—"

"I would have looked after her as my own," the duke agreed, "if I had but known of her plight. As fate would have it, I was abroad for some years and knew nothing of it."

"I was far from this place and unsure of where it lay," the puppeteer said. "In time I grew quite content living on the road, giving shows with my puppets."

"Were you not afraid?" Mouse said.

"Of course I was, at first. But I had lived with Father all my life, so it was easy enough to wear his clothes, to walk and speak as he had. Being alone did not frighten me nearly so much as living as an orphan, at the mercy of strangers."

Sudden guilt washed over Mouse in such a hot,

sickening wave that she thought she might faint. "If only I had told you!" she cried. "I saw Ordin at the ribbon seller's in Marlingford. I asked him to our play. And that day in Wickham, when we ran from those horrid boys and your hood slipped off your hair, he must have seen us then. If you had not been rescuing me—"

"My dear Mouse. This trouble is not of your making," the puppeteer said. "I saw Ordin in Marlingford as we drove into the village and, later, as he watched our play from the back of the crowd. As he made no move to harm us, I was certain he had not recognized me. But then I saw his face at the theater in Reedham while we waited for our permit. His gaze was so full of hate, I knew he had found me out."

"That is why you were so jumpy that day," Mouse said. "You were afraid. Why did you not tell me?"

"I did not wish to alarm you on the eve of your first performance."

"Someone followed me in the crowd that night," Mouse said. "I meant to warn you, but then Simon found us, and I was so happy to see him, I forgot. Oh, I am such an addle brain! This is all my fault."

She bent over the puppeteer's bed. Now that she knew about Ordin, everything else—Alice the goose woman's tale, Simon's story, the puppeteer's nervousness and secrecy—all made sense. Still, she was disappointed her mentor had not trusted her with the truth. "Why did you not tell me sooner?"

"I hoped to keep you safe, little one," the puppeteer said weakly. "For I have grown much fonder of you than I intended."

"That is why you refused me your name, that morning in Marbury Wood."

The puppeteer nodded and tightened her grasp on Mouse's hand.

"Ordin cannot harm us anymore," Mouse said. "When spring comes and you are well, we shall go just where we please, merry as the day is long."

"You must not hope for things that will never be," the puppeteer whispered. "Come closer, Mouse, and do not let go of my hand. Death comes soon."

"The pain makes you speak so!" Mouse cried. "But you must not say such things. I cannot bear it."

"We bear what we must." In the flickering firelight the puppeteer's face was serene. "Will you swear a solemn oath?"

Choking back her sobs, Mouse nodded.

"Look after our dear puppets."

"By all the saints, I do swear it."

"For all their beauty, without your spirit they are naught but bits of wood and paint."

"I will guard their lives as my own," Mouse said.

"Finish our play. Make our jesters dance. And when the people laugh, remember me."

"How can I think of laughter when my heart is broken? I cannot tell our stories without you. It is too soon! I am not ready!"

"You are afraid," the puppeteer whispered hoarsely. "But you will find a way. A kite rises highest against the wind."

The duke turned from the window, his cheeks glistening with tears.

The puppeteer drew a long, shuddering breath. "I leave to you, my dear apprentice, all I have in this world—our wagon and our puppets, my scabbard and sword. And my name, if you would have it."

Mouse bent over the bed once more, her tears falling fast onto the puppeteer's pillow. The puppeteer's breath was but a whisper as she bestowed upon Mouse her final gift.

CHAPTER THIRTEEN

A Beginning

They buried the puppeteer on a rise overlooking the river. Standing with the duke and Lunette as the prayers were read, Mouse recalled the fortune-teller's words: *a long journey, a great sorrow, a dream fulfilled.*

"Ashes to ashes," the priest intoned. "Dust to dust."

Her dream had come true but at much too dear a price. If only the puppeteer might be restored to life, Mouse thought, she would gladly give up everything. But there existed in the world no sorcery or magic stronger than death. Tears ran along the faded scar on her cheek and trickled into the collar of the worn red cloak pulled tightly about her shoulders. Sick with grief, she leaned upon the arm of the stricken duke.

From across the rise came the sound of iron against iron and the rattle of milk pails. Mouse wondered how the smithy and the dairymaids could go on about their chores as if nothing had happened, when her own world had been so completely sundered.

"*Laus Deo* and amen." The priest closed his prayer book and tossed a handful of dirt on the coffin.

Mouse hid her face and sobbed.

The duke placed a reassuring hand on her shoulder. "This seems a cheerless place just now, but when spring comes, I shall plant primroses hereabouts. I shall make a garden for her as long as God grants me breath. Is there naught I can do to ease your grief?"

Lunette slipped her gloved hand into Mouse's bare one. "Father says you may stay here as long as you wish. I hope you stay forever. Oh, say you will, at least till Christmas!"

Mouse stared blankly at the little girl. Fortune had made havoc of all her dreams. What would she do now?

"We are in your debt, my dear, for ridding us of a great menace," the duke said. "You shall want for nothing this house affords for as long as you care to stay. There will be time to think of the future once the winter snows are past."

"Do not be so sad, Mouse," Lunette said. "On the morrow we shall celebrate All Hallows'. Cook will make wassail and Father will take us a-souling."

"We shall have wassail," the duke agreed, "but I do not think it proper to go running about the village begging for sweet cakes while we mourn our puppeteer."

"Oh." Lunette looked crestfallen for a moment, then brightened. "Mayhap you will give a puppet play, Mouse. I should think that would be more exciting than a-souling."

Before the duke could speak, Mouse surprised herself, saying, "Mayhap I will."

The next night after supper, Mouse, the duke, Lunette, Nurse Catchpole, and the serving girl Mouse had met upon her arrival gathered before the fireplace in the dining hall. The wassail cups were passed, and Mouse brought out her puppets.

As she had on the day of her first performance, Mouse spread the blue cloth on the floor and arranged the folds to look like waves on water. Then she brought out Bridget, Sir Alfred, and Noah. After carefully suspending Sir Alfred from the back of a vacant chair, she said, "I shall need an assistant."

She pretended to look about the room, pretended not to see Lunette's small hand waving wildly in the air.

"I will help!" the girl finally cried, and then Mouse showed Lunette how to hold Noah still so his strings would not get tangled.

"Take care," Mouse cautioned, "for he is quite heavy. You must not drop him on his head."

"I will not hurt him," the little girl promised, her eyes shining.

Turning to her small audience, Mouse said, "Without a proper stage, I cannot show the sword. You must use your imaginations and think of it suspended here, in the middle of the water."

The duke smiled and sipped his wassail. The serving girl nodded solemnly. Nurse Catchpole folded her arms across her ample bosom and sniffed. Then Mouse lifted Bridget and walked her to the middle of the lake.

"You cannot get this sword," she said to Sir Alfred, using Bridget's voice.

Then she inserted the *pivetta* into her mouth and gave Sir Alfred's reply. "I know that. As a favor to me, would you give the sword to my lord the king, for there is not in all the world a better use for it."

Lost in her story and in the happy memory of the first performance with her beloved puppeteer, Mouse felt a little better. When the play ended, everyone clapped, even the sour-faced nurse.

"Oh, the puppets are wondrous!" Lunette said, handing Noah carefully to Mouse. "Make us another play!"

"Enough, Lunette," her father said. "To bed with you."

When his daughter had gone, the duke said to Mouse, "It was kind of you to give us a play when your heart is so heavy. Mayhap it will ease your sorrow to know my men have nearly completed repairing your wagon. It will be good as new anon."

"When it is ready to travel, so shall I be." She folded the blue cloth and tucked the *pivetta* back into its small wooden box.

"I can see you are eager for the road," the duke said. "But there cannot be much work for you in the dead of winter. And it is not safe to take a wagon over icy roads. Lunette is right. You must stay till the winter celebrations are past."

And so it was that Mouse remained in Gimingham with the duke and his daughter through Christmas. For days the house rang with the laughter of long-invited guests, who ate too much and drank too much and slept in disheveled heaps on the floor. Greenery hung from the windows and doorways and candles brightened every room. In the courtyard a Yule log blazed merrily through the long winter nights.

Christmas dinner was roasted goose and mince pie. There was wassail and stories and carols that stretched into the afternoon but none of the noisy Christmas games Mouse had so often overheard at Dunston. Instead, the priest returned from the abbey and recited prayers that lasted till sundown.

It was the finest celebration Mouse had ever seen,

but neither the feast nor the musicians' lilting songs nor the priest's prayers could ease her grief. The next day the duke's guests scattered. The men went out riding, and the ladies gossiped and napped. But Mouse could not sleep. Huddled on a stool before the fire in the drafty solar, she stared numbly into the dancing flames, only half listening to Lunette's prattling and Nurse Catchpole's endless chatter.

"Of course, 'tis too bad the puppeteer is dead," the nurse opined, "but what should such a woman expect when she insists on going about the countryside as freely as a man?"

Lunette sipped her wassail. "I should dearly love to travel in a wagon and visit every village in the realm with the puppets for company."

"Ha! As the priest says, fools die for want of wisdom. The only wonder is that the puppeteer was not killed sooner, mingling with other unsavory folk one finds upon the road."

"Your lord the good duke did not find her unsavory," Mouse said, "since it was she who saved his life and thereby preserved the roof that this very night shelters you from the cold."

The nurse opened her mouth to speak, then clamped it firmly shut again. Mouse rose and left the room. On the way to her own bedchamber, she peeked in an open door. The coverlet on the narrow bed was turned down, the curtains were drawn against the winter chill, and a fire burned in the grate. On a small table near the fire lay an open book.

Mouse glanced over her shoulder. The corridor was deserted, so she went in and picked up the book. It felt solid and warm in her hands; she ran her fingers lightly over the pages and inhaled the faint odor of ink.

"I believe this is my room," said the priest from the doorway.

Mouse whirled around. "Oh!"

"Mayhap you wish to borrow my book?"

"I cannot read. It must be very hard to learn, for I have never known anyone who can do it."

"It is not so difficult," he said. "Letters combine to form words, words join to become sentences, sentences grow into paragraphs. It is quite a useful skill for scholars and priests but not of much use for a puppeteer."

Mouse could think of many ways reading could prove useful. Imagine all the new stories her puppets could tell if only she knew how to read! And in every village there were fliers and banners, playbills and posters, all meant to be read. But she would not argue with a holy man. "I must go," she muttered, and made good her escape.

In the hall she met the duke, returning chilled and

red-cheeked from his ride. "Forgive me," he said, removing his scarf and riding gloves. "I could not help overhearing. You must not mind the priest. He has a good heart, but he wears his learning like a crown. Most unbecoming, if I may say so. Have you had any supper?"

"I am not hungry. I drank some wassail with Lunette and Nurse Catchpole."

"Nurse Catchpole? No wonder you have lost your appetite. Not that I am ungrateful for her attention to Lunette since my dear wife died, but by my saints! Her tongue is sharp as a butter woman's."

Mouse grinned despite herself.

"Pay her no mind," the duke continued. "Come now. I am famished, and you must eat as well. You are pale as a winter morn."

When they were seated in the dining hall, he rang for a serving girl, who presently returned with slices of roast goose, a plate of cheese, and wedges of cake. Mouse found that she was quite hungry after all.

"Have you given any more thought to your future?" the duke asked, spearing a morsel of meat. "I would do all in my power to make a goodly home for you here."

"You are kind," Mouse said. "And it is peaceful here."

"But you made a promise to your puppeteer."

Mouse nodded.

"She would not hold you to it, should you decide to stay. Did you not tell me how she herself urged you to find a better life?" He peered across the table at her. "Oh, dear. I have upset you again. We shall speak of other things."

After their meal Mouse hurried to her bedchamber and lifted her puppets from the trunk.

"What shall I do?" she asked Sir Alfred.

But it was Bridget who answered. *What else is there to do but carry on?*

Yes, you must, the sorcerer agreed.

"I do love you all," Mouse said. "But I am afraid."

Afraid? Sir Alfred said. *Where is your courage?*

"Mayhap I never was brave but too addlebrained to recognize danger."

Now you talk nonsense, Bridget said. *Or mayhap it is false modesty that makes you speak so. What of the morn in Marbury Wood? You saved us all then.*

Courage is nothing more than going ahead, even when you feel afraid, Sir Alfred said. *You may take my word on that, for I have made a life of being brave, have I not?*

There came a knock at the door, and in came Lunette in her nightdress. "You are still awake."

Mouse said, "I am awake, but you should be in bed. Your father will not like it if he finds you here so late."

"He is already asleep," the child confided, picking up

the sorcerer. "Can your sorcerer truly do magic? I hope so, for I am in desperate need of a pony, but Father says I am still too young. Will the sorcerer conjure one for me? If he will, I want a bay mare with a white star on her forehead and a shaggy mane for putting ribbons in."

Mouse laughed. "I do not think he makes that kind of magic, but we shall ask him all the same."

Taking the sorcerer from the girl's arms, Mouse said, "If it please you, O sorcerer, give this child a pony. It is a bay mare she wants, with a mane for putting ribbons in."

"Do not forget the white star on her forehead," Lunette prompted.

Mouse held her ear close to the sorcerer's mouth, listened for a moment, then nodded sagely. "Yes. I see."

"What did he say?" Lunette asked, fairly dancing about the room. "I could not hear a single word!"

"He says to ask again when you are ten summers old."

"Ten summers? I will not need his magic then," Lunette said. "This sorcerer is of no use at all!" She perched on the puppets' trunk. "Will you give a play for me, then? I cannot sleep."

"Not now. I am busy making a new play."

"I hope it is a scary one," Lunette said. "I still want a tale of witches and goblins."

"It is not a witches' tale," Mouse said, "but the story of a puppet master and his daughter and their fight against an evil enemy. Bridget will play the daughter. I shall make her a cloak of crimson wool. Sir Alfred will play the brave father, and the sorcerer will be the evil enemy. He already owns a black costume, but he is putting up quite a fuss at having to play so unsavory a character."

Lunette's eyes drifted shut. Mouse roused her and sent her to bed, then climbed beneath her own covers, going over the details in her mind. She must carve a sword for Bridget; mayhap there was still a bit of silver paint in the salvaged pot. And she must practice making the voices with the *pivetta*. Her hands moved in the dark, rehearsing each turn of the puppets' heads, each pull of the strings. She could not think of sleep until everything was clear in her mind, for she was determined that the tale of her puppeteer, every bit as thrilling as the story of St. George and the dragon, would not be forgotten.

At the end of the week, the Christmas guests departed. Through the long winter nights that followed, Mouse busied herself sewing costumes and carving new arms and legs for her mangled puppets. With Lunette as her audience, she practiced her new play.

One night just after Candlemas, when Mouse finished practicing the story of Noah and the ark, Lunette clapped her hands and said, "Will you stay here when spring comes?"

Mouse shook her head. "I must take my puppets to the fairs."

"Father thinks you should stay. I heard him say as much to the priest at Christmas. But Nurse Catchpole says you are a bad influence. Are you?"

Mouse laughed. "Mayhap I am, for I do not know what that means. But Nurse Catchpole need not worry. When winter goes, so will I."

"I will go with you," Lunette said. "Mayhap I will become your apprentice."

"I think not." Mouse took up the scrap of red wool she was making into a new cape for Bridget. "The life of a vagabond is not for a maid like you."

"It is good enough for you," Lunette said.

"I had aught but empty pockets and an empty heart when I ran away from Dunston," Mouse said. "But you are a girl of means. You will marry well and have a dozen children and live a life of endless pleasure."

"A life of boredom, I trow."

"You should learn to read. Surely you would never be bored then. I hope to learn it myself someday. Imagine being able to read poems and stories of great adventures anytime you wished."

Lunette clapped one palm to her forehead. "I would rather swallow a bucket of goose fat! Sometimes Father reads for days on end, then mopes about frowning and muttering to himself. If that is what comes of knowing how to read, I want no part of it." She lifted Bridget and twirled her around. "Will you show me how to make this puppet dance? I would pay you for my lessons."

Mouse smiled. How long ago it seemed since she had begged the puppeteer for the same chance. "I know how you feel, but I could not take payment while a guest in your father's house. Mayhap we can make a bargain instead."

And so it was arranged. Lunette learned to make Bridget walk and turn and perch upon her chair, while Mouse, under the good duke's patient eye, unraveled the mysteries of words and sentences and paragraphs.

"I wish you would reconsider," the duke said on an April morning when Mouse was at last making ready her departure. They were standing in the sunny courtyard where the wagon had been brought. The repairs were finished, the horse outfitted with a new harness. The puppets in their new costumes rested safely inside their trunk. "Lunette has grown quite fond of you, and Nurse Catchpole soon will be too old to keep an eye on her."

"Lunette would tire of me soon enough," Mouse said. "I have not yet learned enough to be a proper companion for her."

"Mayhap that is so. But you know as much as any heart can know of the things that matter most. Courage, friendship, devotion to duty. It is those qualities I wish her to learn."

"If you will pardon my saying so, sir, Lunette needs only to look to her own father for that. Your friendship was aught that saved me these past months. I cannot imagine a better teacher for her."

He laughed. "Undeserved praise, though it warms my heart to hear it. But the truth is, children conspire to learn as little as possible from their own fathers, on principle. Lunette, I fear, is no exception. Is there naught I can say to change your mind?"

"I cannot break a solemn vow," Mouse said quietly. Though a part of her longed to remain at Gimingham, she had no doubt as to where her future lay. "For all its hardships, I would miss the open road."

"You will not be lonely without another soul for company?" the duke asked.

"I have my puppets and the folk who come to see the plays. They are enough company for me."

"Even so, if you change your mind, you may be sure a welcome awaits you here."

"Mayhap I will come back someday, if only for a while."

"Godspeed, then," the duke said. "Have you the sword?"

Mouse nodded.

"Remember, you have but to show it if you ever need help hereabouts and I will send aid straightaway."

"I will remember." Mouse climbed onto the wagon and settled onto the seat.

Then he gave her the book they had used for her reading lessons during the long winter nights. "Mayhap you will find this a pleasant companion and a reminder of your friends at Gimingham."

The sun warmed her shoulders. A gentle breeze stirred the just-washed linen drying in the orchard. Above them the spring sky was a bowl of blue. Despite all Mouse had lost, the world seemed a welcoming place, new and full of promise. She marveled to think that a girl born with nothing at all, not even a name, could by sharp wits and hard work make a place in the world.

"Wait!" Lunette hurried across the courtyard. "I have brought food for your journey, Mouse."

"My thanks, Lunette. But from this day, I am no longer called Mouse. From this day, I am Sabine."

The duke nodded. "Her name suits you."

Lunette said, "Sabine. Mayhap we shall see you at the Midsummer's fair."

"I will look for you there." She handed Lunette a small likeness of the sorcerer she had carved from a scrap of oak. "Keep making wishes," she said. "Sometimes wishes come true."

To the duke she said, "I thank you for all your kindness to me and my puppeteer. God's blessings on your house, my lord."

"And on yours," the duke returned, "though it be a wagon."

Then she snapped the reins, and the wagon rolled through the arched gate and rumbled across the bridge spanning the shining river. When she reached the grassy rise where the puppeteer lay, she halted the horse and jumped down.

Bees buzzed in a patch of thyme, and the nearby sedges rustled in the breeze. Here and there, a few violets peered through the last of the winter stubble. She pulled them carefully from the soil and laid them on the grave.

"Whisper your sorrows to the wind and go forth singing," she said to herself.

A meadowlark sailed by, chirping vigorously. Turning her face to the sun, she closed her eyes and listened. When his song ended, she climbed onto the wagon and flicked the reins.

"Though it be but April," she said to the horse, "I feel like singing a Maysong." She sang as the wagon began to move:

"When first the leaves are green upon the trees,
And bees in the newborn blossoms buzz,
When the sun shines bright and sweet birdsong fills the
   wood,
Then does my heart sing for joy."

The wagon rattled down the rise and across the bright meadow, till the manor house was lost among the trees and all Sabine could see was the road ahead, rising up to meet her.

AUTHOR'S NOTE

Since earliest times people have used puppets in religious ceremonies, for celebrations, education, and entertainment.

During their village festivals, ancient Egyptian women carried images of fertility gods with movable parts to ensure a plentiful harvest. Other Egyptian statues had arms and heads that moved by means of strings, but scholars have no evidence that the Egyptian puppets were used for plays or entertainment. In ancient Greece and Rome, however, actors wearing masks portrayed a number of stock characters—such as Bucco, the comic slave; Maccus, the country bumpkin; and Dossennus, the sharp-tongued hunchback—that later were represented by puppets. Little is known about how the puppets were made, or what materials were used but very old written records provide a few clues.

Written references to puppets in Greece date to the year 421 B.C. And writing in Rome in the year 30 B.C., the poet Horace described men "who are moved like a wooden puppet with wires that pull." From these writings, we know that marionettes, like those Mouse and her puppeteer used, have been around for a long time. Glove puppets were also known in ancient Greece, though we don't know what kinds of plays were performed with them.

For almost eight hundred years, from A.D. 400 to 1200, there are no written records of puppets and puppeteers in Europe, perhaps because the Catholic Church condemned all entertainers. But by the thirteenth century puppeteers were giving plays to entertain the king and queen of France. Plays during this time were often about brave knights and fierce dragons, but there were also religious plays and church services in which puppets were used to dramatize stories from the Bible.

Puppetry soon spread to Italy, where a hunchbacked puppet named Pulcinella entertained audiences and became the model for the English puppet called Punch. Puppeteers and puppetry in England, where our story takes place, fell in and out of fashion over many years. During the sixteenth and seventeenth centuries puppeteers were mostly vagabonds who carried their puppets with them and performed at private houses or at fairs and festivals in small towns. Sometimes they gave their plays out-of-doors. Sometimes they rented theaters, giving as many as nine performances a day, announcing a coming performance by putting up a banner and beating a drum. The upper classes considered these puppet plays to be vulgar and common, but the "ordinary folk"—peasants, laborers, and other artists—flocked to them.

During the eighteenth century London society embraced the puppet theater, and for many years the wealthy attended elaborately staged shows In elegant theaters while the less fortunate continued to enjoy street plays and open-air performances. But tastes in entertainment, much like tastes in fashion, are ever-changing, and by the end of the century the puppet show had once again fallen out of favor.

History records at least two female puppeteers in England. In creating my fictional puppeteer, I borrowed a few traits from one of them, a young woman named Charlotte Charke who dressed in men's clothing and for a time ran one of the most successful puppet theaters in England. Charlotte was the youngest daughter of an actor and poet named Colley Cibber. She began her theatrical career as an actress and in 1738 mounted an ambitious puppet show in London that included plays by William Shakespeare and ballad operas by Henry

Fielding. Later, she took her theater on the road, performing in Tunbridge Wells, but the tour was unsuccessful and she returned to London and rented her show to a man named Yeates. Eventually, she fell on hard times and was forced to sell her marionettes and scenery, but she is described as a puppeteer of unusual intelligence, taste, and courage.

Today, the ancient art of puppetry is kept alive through performances sponsored by puppet guilds and through exhibits in museums. Puppeteers of America, established in 1937, charters puppetry guilds across the country and sponsors a National Day of Puppetry each April. Their official magazine, *Puppetry Journal,* features the work of American puppeteers and puppet makers.

The Center for Puppetry Arts in Atlanta, Georgia, carries on an active program of education and performance and maintains a museum and a reference library. The Ballard Institute and Museum of Puppetry at the University of Connecticut at Storrs features the work of puppeteers and puppet makers from around the world and offers studies in the art and craft of puppet theater. In Italy the International Museum of Marionettes Antonio Pasqualino in Palermo conducts workshops and seminars for teachers and children, maintains a reference library, and mounts exhibits both there and abroad.

My own fascination with puppets began when I was a child, watching television shows featuring marionettes. To me, the marionettes seemed to have distinct personalities of their own, and I delighted in their interactions with the humans on the shows. A few years ago, while browsing in a library, I came across a book about the history of the English puppet theater. Even before I finished reading the book, I knew I would have to write a novel about the world of the traveling puppeteers. *The Puppeteer's Apprentice* is the result. I hope you enjoyed reading it as much as I enjoyed writing it.

BIBLIOGRAPHY

Cosman, Madeline. *Medieval Word Book*. New York: Facts on File, 1996.

Dyer, Christopher. *Standards of Living in the Later Middle Ages: Social Change in England, 1200–1520*. Cambridge: Cambridge University Press, 1989.

Gies, Frances, and Joseph Gies. *A Medieval Family*. New York: HarperCollins, 1998.

————. *Life in a Medieval Castle*. New York: Harper and Row, 1974.

Goodrich, Norma Lorre. *Merlin*. New York: Harper Perennial, 1988.

Morgan, Kenneth, ed. *The Oxford Illustrated History of Britain*. Oxford: Oxford University Press, 1984.

Speaight, George. *The History of the English Puppet Theater*. New York: John DeGraff, 1955.